Hotdog Down

A Denise Reed Mystery

by

Mary Koppel

For information, email Cozy Cat Press, cozycatpress@aol.com or visit our website at: www.cozycatpress.com

COZY CAT
P R E S S

ISBN: 978-1-946063-58-8

Printed in the United States of America

10 9 8 7 6 5 4 3 2 1

Dedication

First of all, writing this Denise Reed mystery has been such a treat. A few years ago, when I was between positions, I was an extra in a movie being filmed in New Orleans. The process was so interesting to me. Who knew that a five minute scene that ended up on an editing room floor could take so long to produce?

During that same time, between positions, I spent some quality time at PJ's Coffee Shops in New Orleans. At one shop, I met a kind and funny woman who inspired the character of Lacy. Only later would I appreciate the lesson she taught me: perhaps I needed some time between positions to really pay attention to the gifts all around me. I don't know this woman's last name but I'm thankful for her words that day.

I am grateful for the support and strength of my wonderful family: my mother, my sisters, my brothers-in-law, my brother and sister-in-law, my nieces and nephews. I am especially grateful to my daughter and Naomi Keith who watched her while I finished writing.

Finally, I dedicate this book to the congregation at All Saints' Episcopal Church in Miami, Oklahoma. Thank you!

I hope you enjoy *Hot Dog Down*, A Denise Reed Mystery!

Chapter 1

"Are you comfortable?" Claudia, the casting director, asked me while two burly "handlers" forcibly yanked a six-foot long hotdog costume over my head. Was she insane? Of course, I wasn't comfortable. Two massive workmen with tree trunks for arms shoved, pulled and wiggled the costume on me. Sweat was already dripping down my leg. At last, my face popped through the opening, my brown hair covering my eyes.

"There you are!" Claudia looked at me and smiled with such sweetness that I bit back my response. Screaming and strangling her would be wrong and, in this costume, probably impossible. I was dressed as a six-foot long Lucky Dog hotdog, complete with ketchup, mustard, and old sweat stains from the costume's previous guest. My two "handlers" inspected the costume again, nodded to each other and walked away.

"How lucky for us that you fit perfectly in that costume!" Claudia exclaimed. "You and Ellis must be about the same size; of course, he doesn't have hips." She said the last part with a gleam in her eyes. She pulled a makeup case from under her arms and, with a brush, blotted red powder on my face. "Now your skin won't clash with the color of the dog." Great. I was a hippy, pasty-faced hotdog.

Claudia pushed the hair from my eyes, tucking it into the opening of the costume. Then she handed me two enormous white gloves. As she helped slip them on my hands, she went on: "For this scene, Denise, I need you to dance like a hotdog while the brass band is playing." Dance like a hotdog? How do you dance like a hotdog?

She turned me around to face a full-length mirror. I had some idea what I might look like, but it was much worse than what I'd imagined. I was a six-foot long wiener with a face so red it looked like someone had squirted me with ketchup. I noticed some sort of brownish yellow stain right below my waistline that looked suspiciously like some poor soul had not make it to the port-o-potty in time. The whole image was frightening.

She took hold of my arm and led me around to the back of a trailer. She held my arm with an unexpectedly tight grip. At last, she stopped right in the middle of Bourbon Street. On the ground was an "X" made from black duct tape directly in front of a black gymnastics mat. She continued speaking: "You need to stay on the "X", right about here, so when Charles hits you; you'll land on the mat and not get hurt. Got it?" Again, she smiled sweetly. I nodded as best I could and then her words registered.

"Wait. Did you say someone is going to hit me or kiss me?" Claudia let out a chortle of laughter that I am sure revealed that the woman was an actual jackal from hell in skinny taupe jeans, horn-rimmed glasses, and a gold seashell pendant necklace. She scooted me forward to my spot and then walked away giggling.

I marveled at all that was going on around me. The film company with its trailers and crew must have taken over at least two or three square blocks in the French Quarter. Trailers lined one block of Royal Street and one side of Bourbon. The two streets that connected Bourbon and Royal were filled with costumers, boom microphones, wires and all sorts of strange equipment. The whole set-up was impressive.

I looked around at the other movie extras. The scene was a crowded Mardi Gras celebration on Bourbon Street, except it was November and between takes the group was entirely too quiet. Some extras were dressed as clowns or wore colorful masks. I noticed a few dressed as silly animals. Two or three men wore grass skirts and, of course, all the other women were dressed in sexy costumes. I was dressed as a hotdog. My big screen debut would be as a hotdog in the latest Michael Murphy-directed action comedy.

One might ask me: how does a 30 something, mildly overweight, divorced mother of one with two degrees end up as a wiener standing alone on Bourbon Street? The question seems fair enough. I was asking it myself. Perhaps I've always been asking myself that question my whole life. Okay, that's over dramatic. I suppose that's my own fault.

My name is Denise Reed. I am 34 years old, divorced and the mother of the most amazing four-year-old named Emily. I love to read. I like helping people. I'm curious too. I'm also freaking out just a little bit.

About six months ago, I talked myself out of my position as a youth and family ministry coordinator at a large church in New Orleans. While I was good at what I did at the church, I was becoming unhappy with my work there. I was not exactly sure why.

I guess after my daughter entered my life, I started thinking differently about what I did and who I wanted to be. Perhaps I didn't really like my ex-boss, the pompous Rev. Foucher. Maybe I was destined for greater things. Or somehow I was not seeing how sitting in another meeting discussing how we could advocate for the less fortunate as the same as actually helping the less fortunate.

Don't get me wrong. Some parts of my old job were great. I would visit with folks, encourage them to participate in church activities, and arrange outreach opportunities for families. I liked when I was helping people. I liked when I could encourage people to help people. I also liked the time I spent with the youth of the church. I ate a lot of pizza with 10-year-olds.

Still, I felt like I could do more. I had ideas for new ministries that I thought would be helpful and meaningful. I would share them with my boss and he would say to "keep to the glorified babysitting." One afternoon while meeting with my ex-boss I shared that I was unhappy with the position and maybe I needed to do something else. My ex-boss agreed and encouraged me to find out what that was something else was.

I left the position with a lot of bravado, thinking that I'd explore just what God was calling me to do and possibly walk into a new position at another church in town. Instead, a new position did not materialize. In a matter of weeks, I was freaking out because it definitely was not an "Eat, Pray, Love" kind of decision.

For the first month or so, I hid. I was embarrassed and unsure. My confidence was shot and financially I was not quite in the right place for an extended vacation. Honestly, I was not sure what you are supposed to do with a lot of free time. I don't think it should be called "free time" at all. The time isn't actually free. Perhaps it should be called "not free" time.

My friends had encouraged me to think about this time differently. I should have seen not working full time as an opportunity. I should have counted my blessings. I knew I should have, but it wasn't easy. I should have welcomed the time so that I could use it to learn about the world around me and myself. All I was really learning was that I really stunk at not having full time employment. I felt desperate. Frankly, I was only seeing it as an opportunity to starve to death!

Of course, things had kind of been working out or at least things were interesting. My daughter and I started living with my mother to save money. Her house is a beautiful renovated Double Shotgun-style home right near the Whole Foods on Magazine Street in New Orleans. Being near a good grocery store can be a bonus. Plus, Mom has a great front porch swing that my daughter loves.

While I had been driving my mother nuts, she really enjoyed doting on my daughter, who's amazing. Emily was going into pre-school and she's always ready to give a hug and a kiss. She looks like a mini version of Audrey Hepburn, especially if I put her hair in a ponytail. I had that going for me.

My mother started pushing me to get out of the house. While I've been reluctant to admit it, she'd been right (really the question is when is she ever wrong?). So I began to go to Latter Library almost every day to write cover letters and send out resumes. Half the time, I perused the Mystery and Romance section upstairs, but my mother didn't need to know about that part. At least, I was out of the house.

Thanks to my mother's loving push, I had even started volunteering with her. That volunteering led to a part-time job. Most recently, I had worked at a luxury nursing home where I'd figured out who was stealing from its residents and solved an actual mystery. That was cool. I wouldn't have been able to do that if I was still working full time. The whole experience there did give me a shot of much needed confidence.

Of course, eventually the nursing home reduced my hours. They were "restructuring positions." So, I was back to sending out more resumes and having a lot of time on my hands, but I was not feeling as bad about it as I was before. I think I have been figuring out my purpose and my gifts. I like to help people, so I have been trying to figure out how I can do that as a career option. Not a lot of superhero gigs available though. I also look pretty silly in tights.

So in my push to get out of the house, expand my horizons, and learn something, I had taken on some odd jobs. I would do a few things here and there that would still afford me time to send out my resume. Right around Christmas, I even promised someone I would cat sit. Yep, I was exploring new horizons, resume building—not.

A few weeks ago, one of my closest friends, Carrie Boudreaux, asked for help with her screenplay (her script is amazing, by the way). We had been talking about it and how to break into Hollywood. My suggestion was a crazed cross county road trip and sneaking into a Hollywood studio.

Instead, Carrie read an ad on Craigslist looking for extras for a movie. She thought she could do some research about movie production while there. I still thought my idea was pretty good, but our clandestine, cross country sneaking would have to wait. She was supposed to be off from work this week. I wasn't working this week. So we signed up. Of course, Carrie works as a lawyer and got called into the office at the last minute so I went alone.

I guess it wasn't all bad. When I arrived at the shoot, the casting director offered me an additional $50 a day if I would wear the hotdog costume. Of course, at the time, she didn't mention getting knocked over in it. Nor did she mention how rude people are to a woman dressed as a hotdog on Bourbon Street in New Orleans. People have some strange fetishes in this city.

I heard the director shout what I could only assume was "action" and the brass band began to play. I tried to dance which amounted to me rocking back and forth and flapping my arms. I could hear some laughter, but I continued until the director shouted "cut."

I could feel someone tap my back as I shifted around. Claudia, the casting director, smiled and shook her head. "The director needs you to really dance. You know, go ahead and cut loose! He said that you look like you're just having a seizure right now. Okay?" She pushed back her tiny glasses and swung around. She shouted something to a few of the other extras. A few scantily clad women walked closer, holding their glasses of faux hurricanes.

Once again, the music started up. I really tried to move. I thought I was getting the hang of it when I leaned a little too much into a shimmy and down I went. Once again, I heard the director shout "cut!" I could hear some type of swearing and murmuring coming from the direction of the camera. My two handlers walked over, each took one of my arms and lifted me. Again, I watched Claudia approach. She whispered into her cellphone and pressed the off button. She absently pulled at her seashell necklace, moving the pendant along the chain back and forth. She plastered on an annoyed smile.

"Okay, Denise, that was okay, but you really need to give it your all." I could see that Claudia was getting aggravated, "Just think of one of those blow-up guys you see flailing around in front of a used car lot? Got it!" I nodded and smiled.

Once again, I heard the brass band play. I began my wild flailing. I tried not to look at anyone else as I shook, but every now and then I caught the eye of one of the other extras. The woman immediately put her hand over her mouth to control her laughter. I turned away and immediately felt my feet rise up and I started flying backwards with a huge man on top of me.

We landed on the ground with a thud. The man knocked the wind out of me. When I finally opened my eyes, I looked up into the most beautiful clear blue eyes I have ever seen, familiar blue eyes. Dreamy blue eyes peeked out beneath a prominent and rugged brow. I grunted under the weight of that solid, muscular frame. I knew that body. It was attached to Chase Clarke, the American version of Hugh Jackman. Oh my gosh! Chase Clarke, film superstar, was on top of me!

All I could do was squeak out: "You're crushing my pelvis, I think!" I released a pent up breath into the man's perfectly chiseled face. His serious expression broke and he smiled. His teeth were so straight and white! I could feel the man shake as he tried to control his laughter. Hey, I might have a broken bone, but I made Chase Clarke laugh.

"Cut!" This time I could hear the director's shout. "What was that?" he exclaimed. I could hear the clattering of a chair falling over and arguing.

Chase Clarke stayed in place on top of me and looked from side to side. He waved over one of the members of the crew. In a stage whisper he asked, "How did I look? Was my hair okay?" The crewmen nodded approvingly. With that, the Adonis of the Silver Screen rolled off me and I began rocking back and forth until my handlers arrived.

I watched the backside of the actor I knew so well. Tight dark jeans, a perfectly clean white t-shirt hid his muscular perfection. Someone with a hairbrush and hairspray ran over to him and began grooming him. My admiration was interrupted by the director, a short man in a Kinks' t-shirt, green ball cap and jeans. He stomped straight up to me. He threw down his clip board and tapped his tiny foot at me.

I think he was trying to be really intimidating, but the end result was like having a Keebler elf try to look tough. What was he going to do to me? Punish me by baking oatmeal raisin cookies? Actually, that would be awful, especially if you preferred chocolate chip and he showed up with oatmeal raisin. I looked down at the grouchy elf, still smarting from my fall and trying to contain my laughter.

We both stood staring at each other. Clearly he expected me to say something, but I was not going to say a word. He put his hands on his hips (dare I say it again, tiny hips?). The set was quiet. Something told me that this must have happened often.

"Hotdogs do not talk!" He spoke through gritted teeth. A tiny bit of spittle gathered in the corner of his mouth.

"They do if you squish them," I replied. I could hear a murmur of giggles coming from somewhere around me, but I did not have peripheral vision in my costume. His head swung from side to side, looking for the offenders.

"Do you know who I am?" he asked indignantly. His chest was heaving "I have directed over thirty films. I have two Oscar nominations for Best Picture. One Golden Globe. Who do you think you're talking to? Why are you even talking?"

I shifted to look at him straight on. I had at least four inches on this guy and maybe 20 pounds. Yep, I was shaking in my hotdog—not. What was he going to do? Fire me? Been there, done that. Actually, as I thought about it, I smiled.

Right there on Bourbon Street I was having an epiphany. I was sweating like a pig at a barbecue. I definitely had a bruise on my bottom. I realized that getting fired right at that moment might not be so bad. That possibility really didn't hold as much fear for me as it had in the past. I guess things were looking up.

At this point, the director was about to explode, especially when I realized I had a ridiculous grin. I cleared my throat and scowled at him. I attempted to put my hands on my hips, mirroring his posture, but my arms couldn't reach. Instead I kind of flailed them and settled on trying to lace my fingers together except I was unable to because of the enormous white gloves. From my left, the giggles became a louder and the whole crew roared with laughter.

I held my scowl as long as I could, but I smiled at the director. He pursed his lips together and turned on his heels and stomped away. I watched Claudia pick up the clip board and chase after the angry little man. I looked to see where the laughter had begun and there was my hero, Chase Clarke! I attempted a curtsy and promptly fell over. Thankfully my handlers were nearby.

Someone announced that we had a break. After all the excitement, I really needed some water and a pee break. I began a slow waddle toward the snack table and port-a-potties. From behind the barricades on Bourbon Street, I heard a hiss and a low, "Hey, sexy hotdog!"

I rolled my eyes and kept moving towards the table. "Hey, hey, wait up a minute!" I turned ready with a harsh rebuke to find a scantily clad young woman approaching me. She smiled broadly at me. "You were so funny! I just wanted to tell you that." She just stood in front of me for a moment. "Wow! Your face is really red. Is that makeup?" She peered a little closer at my cheeks.

I tried to touch my face, but my arms wouldn't reach. "Yes, it's makeup. My name's Denise. What's your name?" I reached forward and shook her hand. She giggled as my gloved hand swallowed her hand.

"My name is Lacy. Have you been in a lot of movies, uh, I mean films? You're so natural," she asked as we wandered to the snack table. I was sure there was nothing natural about being a hotdog. I looked closer at Lacy. She was almost painfully thin and despite the heavy make-up and revealing outfit, she appeared very young.

I smiled at her. "This is my first one, and judging from the director's response, probably my last one." I turned to look in the direction where the Keebler elf incident had occurred. We both giggled. Lacy reached for a bottle of water and handed it to me.

"I wouldn't worry too much about him. He's all macho. That's all for show. He's a sweetheart." She waved her hand dismissively in his direction. Somehow, I was not sure that I agreed with her sentiment about the grumpy elf.

"I love movies. I want to be an actress, but I have to hone my craft. I just started doing a few plays, but it's hard to find gigs, you know?" she said thoughtfully between sips of water. She shook her head like she was thinking about her craft. I shook my head in response. I was not sure if she was joking, but she was serious.

"I like movies too. I'm not really working right now, so this is a fun way to pass the time," I shared and she smiled again. She grabbed a bag of chips from the table and tore it open.

"Me too. I'm only working part-time right now. My boyfriend is working on the movie, so he got me this part. I actually worked all this week." We continued to walk the length of the snack table and as she handed me different snacks, since my arms would not reach. She pointed to two chairs at the end of the table. I attempted to sit, but the costume wouldn't bend.

"So, what does your boyfriend do on the movie, I mean, film?" I looked around at the gathered crew, wondering who this young man might be. She looked back and forth and waved me a little closer.

"I'm not allowed to tell. He's pretty important. We just started dating." She giggled quietly. I giggled too, but had no idea why she was laughing. I looked around again and wondered who it might be. "Of course, also, he's getting divorced, so you know."

I mouthed an "Oh." I wanted so much to say something, but I bit my tongue. We stood in silence for a little bit. I wracked my brain for another question, something to shift the topic from uncomfortable romantic choices.

"So, when you aren't here, what do you do?" Her brown eyes widened at the question and she shifted uncomfortably. Clearly, I picked an even more uncomfortable topic of conversation. I leaned in, as much as a hotdog can lean in and listened.

"Well, I spend a lot of time hanging out, getting coffee and watching people…" She paused and drew in a breath "I'm a dancer." I nodded, but it took me a moment to register what she was saying. She blushed a little and I realized that she felt embarrassed.

"Oh," I answered. I looked at her expression. I had the feeling she had probably experienced a lot of judgment about her work. Before I could even stop myself, I blurted out, "What's it like?"

She looked surprised at my question. "It is what it is. I kind of have to close myself off. It is acting, really. A lot of the girls can't do it, you know. You can get wrapped up in the life. You have to be strong not to." Earlier I thought she seemed very young and naive, but after listening to her, she seemed weary and older.

Lacy went on, even more quietly, "I have a little girl." She bit her lower lip and looked back at me, almost daring me to say something. She seemed to become a little angry, squaring her shoulders.

I wasn't sure what to say so I said the first thing that popped into my head. "I have a little girl too." Her shoulders immediately relaxed and a big smile broke out across her face.

"She's in first grade. She's already in the Alpha reading group." I didn't know what the "Alpha Reading Group" was but I knew maternal pride when I saw it.

"That's wonderful!" I said and our conversation continued. We immediately launched into a lively discussion about local free activities for children. I was surprised about all that she knew, but then chastised myself for the assumptions I had made at her revelation about her romantic life and line of work.

"What did you do before you became a dancing hotdog?" Lacy asked abruptly. The question was innocent and in most cases could be answered simply and easily, but somehow I was not sure how to answer.

I let out a breath, "I used to work at a church. I led the youth and young family ministries, but ..." I kind of let the end of the sentence drift off.

"But what?" she pressed, turning her head as she looked at me. Now it was my turn to feel uncomfortable.

"I lost the job. I was at loose ends, not sure what I wanted to do, and then I told that to my former boss, like an idiot. I talked myself out of the job, said that maybe I needed to be somewhere else. I guess I still feel pretty stupid about the whole thing. I don't know what to do with myself with all this time. I just need to work!" I blurted out the story and she squeezed the water bottle in her hand and wrinkled her forehead in thought.

"I know about stupid mistakes," she said with a mirthless laugh. We both were quiet. I wondered what her life must be like. I bet she'd made a few mistakes. She went on, "Have you ever thought that maybe you need this time?" I was shocked by her profound question.

"For what?" I asked earnestly. She shrugged her shoulders.

"Maybe to make people like me laugh?" I scowled at her and then smiled. I turned back to the snack table and managed to grab a bag of sun chips. I ripped the bag open and the whole thing exploded and fell to the ground. She covered her mouth to keep from laughing.

I looked down at the crumbs and thought about the last few months. I certainly worried about when I would find another position. I agonized about time, but I had never thought that I might need the time for something. What was the purpose of this time?

I tried to dust a few crumbs off my costume, but my hands could not reach. "I just don't know what to do with myself." I almost whispered the words. I could feel a lump growing in my throat.

"Maybe this is a time for learning. You can use this time to observe life, learn something new? I don't know." Lacy words were so profound. She patted my white glove. This woman was not quite who I thought her to be.

"I feel like I've been sending out my resume constantly and nothing seems to stick, but then I wonder why I even bother. Should I even go back to working in a church?" I lamented, "Right now, I'm pretty much doing odd jobs. Twiddling my thumbs."

Lacy looked down at the enormous gloves on my hands and then looked at me. "You're definitely not twiddling your thumbs here. Just look at those things. It must be meant to be!" I lifted my hands and examined the gloves in front of me. Maybe she was right?

"Hey, do you want to see a picture of my daughter?" she asked brightly. I nodded enthusiastically. Clearly, I was not getting a snack, at least not in this outfit.

Maybe instead, I could enjoy this delightful woman's company and pictures. If there is one thing I enjoy, besides my daughter, chocolate, mystery novels, cuddly animals and champagne, it is pictures of people's children. The world needs more pictures of happy children I think!

She stood up and brushed an invisible crumb from her costume. "I left my phone in my car. I think we have time. I actually parked on Dauphine Street. We can just walk down and come back." She leaned in again. "I'm also dying for a cigarette, but I'm not allowed to smoke on set and in my costume." She put her index finger against her lips.

I followed behind her as we wandered a little ways down Bourbon Street, turning onto Bienville, past Arnaud's Restaurant. My stomach grumbled in response to the heavenly odors. Drunks along the way shouted unmentionable things to me about hotdogs as we hurried along. We finally turned onto Dauphine and walked to the middle of the block, stopping at a small rusty Toyota. In one smooth motion, Lacy opened the car's trunk and lit a cigarette while she retrieved her phone.

She handed me her phone. The picture was adorable. A sweet brown-haired girl sat serenely on stool in a familiar blue and white school uniform. Lacy took a long drag from her cigarette and leaned against her car.

"She's so cute," I cooed. Lacy was clearly pleased with my assessment. "Wait, does she go to St. Mary's Episcopal School?" She nodded enthusiastically. "My daughter goes to the pre-school there!"

"Really?" Lacy asked brightly. She dropped her cigarette and stomped on it. She quickly lighted another and took a drag, "I love that place. Thank goodness my parents and ex help. I wish they went to 12th grade." We both nodded our heads. St. Mary's School on Carrollton was absolutely darling. The teachers and students were kind. They emphasized creativity.

"I wish the same thing. Everything about it is wholesome and sweet." I thought about how Emily's teacher had them make the cutest collages. I could tell from Lacy's expression that she must have been thinking about something similar.

"I know," she replied as she tapped ash from the end of her cigarette. She gingerly took the phone from me and swiped through a few more pictures and showed me another. I looked again at the child, this time in a pink tutu and her hair in a slick bun.

"Hey, let's take a selfie. Cecelia will love it, and I bet your daughter will too!" She held the phone out and angled it downward towards us. She pressed the button twice and handed the phone back to me.

"Aww," I answered automatically. I turned a little away from Lacy so I wouldn't breathe in the cigarette smoke and looked at the picture. I looked ridiculous, but Lacy was right. Emily would giggle with delight when she saw it. I swung around quickly toward her to hand her the phone, but I lost my balance and fell flat on my face. I was sure that would result in a bruise. I lay face down on Dauphine Street a moment and then began to rock back and forth trying to flip over.

I heard Lacy laugh. "A little help here, please!" I called from the ground. I waved my arms; sure that Lacy would grab hold of me. I kept trying to roll over, but my hands were too far out from each other to push myself up and over. I kept rocking. All at once, Lacy stopped laughing.

I could hear shoes running up alongside me. And then I heard Lacy gasp. I heard feet scraping and what sounded like someone tearing clothing.

"Leave me alone! You're hurting me! Let go!" Lacy growled to the other person. I couldn't really see. I tried holding myself up. Finally I got enough momentum and I flipped myself over, but I was now flat on the ground. From my peripheral vision, I could see Lacy and someone struggling. I could just see the individual in silhouette.

"Stop it! Let go of me!" She tried to pull away but the person pulled her close to him and I watched as Lacy slumped and collapsed to the ground. For a moment, the person looked in my direction. He wore a hoody that concealed his face. It seemed like he lacked any features but I noticed that the cuff of the attacker's sleeve was frayed, two strings stuck out from his cuff. I also could see he held a knife. He took a step towards me and I released a scream that would have straightened Shirley Temple's hair.

Chapter 2

Two hours later, I was freed from my hotdog prison and sat curled up on the couch in my mother's living room. My mother tucked a comforter around me and turned on the news. I thought back to earlier in the evening. I had been so hot and now I was chattering.

Thankfully, the police had arrived a few minutes after the attack. I guess they scared off the attacker, but they didn't catch him. I spent the next hour answering questions as the police processed the scene and an ambulance took Lacy away. Her prognosis did not sound good.

I tried to shake the incident from my mind, but I kept seeing Lacy struggle and then slump to the ground. I didn't realize I was thinking about it so intently until my mother's voice jolted me: "Here's your hot cocoa!"

I looked up at my mother. She held out a flowery mug toward me. A crease grew between her eyes as she smiled down at me. I could tell she wanted to say something, but she pressed her lips together.

"Thanks, Mom," I took the mug and sipped the perfectly warmed liquid. I was pretty sure she hadn't added sugar, but I smiled reassuringly at her.

She sat next to me and protectively put an arm around me. I felt suddenly warm and safe. Thank God for Mom!

"You really scared the you-know-what out of me," she said matter of factly. My mother hardly ever cursed. I turned to look at her in her usual pressed blue polo and pearls. Her short brown hair was tucked neatly behind her ears adorned with small pearl studs. Her makeup from the day was now gone, but she still looked fresh. Margaret Reed, my mother, was usually so calm, every hair and every stich in place, but tonight I could tell she was rattled.

My mother sighed heavily. She didn't do that often. Usually she was take charge, full of energy and ready to go. She'd retired about five years ago from real estate, but she hadn't slow down one bit. Every morning, she walked two miles with her best friend Marilyn. Next she headed off to some volunteer activity. She spent her afternoons reading, maybe an exercise class or more volunteering. The whole time she was dressed in business casual perfection. She leaned into the couch and turned towards me.

"I was pretty scared too, Mom. We were just talking about our children and she was showing me her pictures. I fell over and then I could hear them struggling and then she went down..." I just stopped talking. I could feel tears well up in my eyes. I prayed silently that Lacy was okay. I wondered about her little girl tonight. I cleared my throat, "How was Emily?"

My mother smiled and shook her head. "Emily was just fine this evening. She negotiated five books. I got her down from seven. I think that I might return to real estate and make her my partner." We both laughed, relieved with the subject change. We both grew quiet. I let out a sigh and shifted.

I looked at the chair next to the couch where a plastic grocery bag sat. It held my personal items from the crime scene, not that I had really anything. Now that I thought about it, I wondered what was in the bag that the sweet police officer had handed me as I'd left the French Quarter. Someone from the movie had already handed me my clothing and purse. What was in this bag?

I stood up and grabbed the bag. Of course, the giant white gloves were there, but it still felt a little too heavy. I reached in and pulled out Lacy's phone.

"Mom! This is her phone!" I looked at it like it might explode. My mother's eyes widened as she hopped from the couch and came to inspect the item. She carefully took the phone from my hand and turned it in her own, pressing down on the home button. The screen immediately lit up with a picture of Lacy and her daughter blowing kisses to the camera.

"Hmm… cute picture." She pressed the home button again, and the screen was suddenly filled with apps. "Not much security," my mother murmured. She tapped on the phone icon, pulling up Lacy's contact list.

"Mom! That's her phone. We can't look through it!" My mother raised one perfectly shaped eyebrow. She looked back down at the phone and began scrolling. "Wait. What are you doing?"

"Denise, I'm not snooping. I'm merely attempting to find her mother's phone number so we can return this phone," my mother retorted. I think she said something under her breath, but I couldn't hear her. I scooted next to her and watched over her shoulder as she scrolled.

I could sense my mother getting frustrated. It seemed just about every name was either an initial or only first names. Who knew there were so many spellings of Becky? My mom released a sigh and handed the phone to me.

"I know there's some way to look up emergency contacts, but she doesn't have anyone's name in there. I thought for sure she'd have someone in there," my mother announced with a huff. "I don't even think she has an Apple id set up!"

I kept scrolling. The names meant nothing to me and offered no clues as to who Lacy's mother might be, for that matter, who her emergency contact was either.

Heck, I, too, couldn't even find a last name. I clicked the phone off. I felt too tired to keep trying. My energy leaked from my body and left me aching.

We both returned to the couch and sat, putting the phone on the arm of the couch. I shook my head. I was exhausted from the evening and angry. I stood up and stretched. "I'm going to sleep, Mom."

"Okay, sweetie. I hope you can get that picture out of your head and rest." She took hold of my hand and squeezed. I nodded. I hoped I could forget the image as well.

I padded down the hallway and peeked into my daughter's room. A small night light illuminated her bed. One little hand rested on her pillow and the other held a brown bear in her arms. I slipped closer to the bed and kissed her forehead. Now I could rest.

Chapter 3

After a fitful night of tossing and turning, I awoke around 7:45 a.m. I knew it was precisely that time because I could hear my mother hustling Emily out the front door with the stage whispered announcement: "Hurry up, Emily! It's 7:45! We have to go!"

I heard Emily demand: "But is it a real hotdog? How are you going to put it in the refrigerator?" I couldn't hear my mother's response. Emily posed a valid point. How would you fit a giant hotdog in a refrigerator?

I closed my eyes again and when I opened them, my mother stood over me. She smiled serenely. I flung an arm over my eyes, "Yes, Mom? Aren't you dropping off Emily?" I pushed myself up and looked for my daughter.

"I already dropped her off. Get dressed; let's go have breakfast!" She patted my arm and turned on her heel. I looked over at the clock. Indeed I had fallen back to sleep for about thirty minutes. I pushed off the covers and headed for the bathroom.

As soon as I stepped into the bathroom, I glanced into the mirror and almost screamed. My face looked like I'd placed it in a microwave oven. I quickly scrubbed the red makeup off my face, thankful that it actually came off. After pulling my hair back, I slipped on a roomy pair of jeans and navy sweater.

I slid into the front seat of my mother's car and she looked over. I could tell she was resisting the urge to straighten something on me. Finally, she reached over and tucked in the label on my sweater. She started the engine and off we drove.

We drove silently all the way to Bywater. At last we arrived at Elizabeth's Restaurant. The eclectic café was located right across from the Mississippi River levy in what must have been an old store. Because it was a little later in the morning, we were seated immediately.

The restaurant was alive with color. Every spot seemed to radiate energy. My mother drew in a breath and beamed. They seated us under a chalkboard menu.

My mother discretely pulled out her glasses and scanned the specials. I perused the menu. I thought about the last time she and I had actually had a meal together without my daughter. It had to have been right before I lost my position at St. Christopher's.

"What are you thinking about, Denise?" my mother asked as she blew on her coffee. "I can tell by your wrinkled forehead that something is worrying you." My mother could always see right through me.

"I guess I was thinking about the last time we went out to eat together. You and I had lunch at Café Degas right before I lost my job." My mother sipped her coffee and thought for a moment.

"No, that can't be right. We have gone to Slice and lots of other places," she argued. She put down her cup and I could see that she was trying to list the places on her fingers.

"I mean just you and me." With that explanation, she opened her mouth promptly, then closed it. She nodded. "I just cannot believe it has been so long and we even live in the same house." My mother examined me from across the table.

"These have been some rough days." My mother spoke softly.

"That's an understatement!" I almost spit out my iced tea in response. Now my mother's brow wrinkled.

"Yes, yesterday was awful, but you know what I mean. I know that losing the position has been a real blow to your self-worth. I also know living with me, as an adult, cannot be easy." At that, I couldn't look at my mother. She was right.

Yesterday's attack on Lacy aside, I felt like I was struggling. I would send out resumes and cover letters and then either hear nothing or "no thank you." At the same time, I wondered if I still wanted to even work in a church. I had always worked there in one form or another.

Only a month or so before, my mother had recommended that I start trying to find a job, just to keep busy. Probably also to keep me out of her hair. I looked across at her.

"Mom, I don't even know what to do. I just need to work, but I wonder if I should stop looking at different church positions and do something else," I answered and wiped a tear from the corner of my eye. My mother reached across the table and took my hand.

"Don't get me wrong, Denise; working is great. It can keep you busy, give you a sense of accomplishment, but it isn't everything. You know that, right?" My mother leaned her head to the side as she asked. Her short brown hair falling from behind her ear. She leaned closer to the table. "What do you like to do? What do you want to do?"

I took a sip of my tea and thought about her question. "I like to help people." My answer made my mother smile.

"There you go! That's what you need to be doing!" She looked back up at the chalkboard menu and folded her hands in front of her, ready to order.

"But, what does that mean? Should I try to find something totally new? Should I keep sending out resumes to churches?" She took off her glasses and tucked them into her pocket. She straightened in her chair.

"Of course you should keep sending out resumes to churches! But you should also look for places where you feel like you can help people. There are a lot of places where you can help. Like when you helped at Riverview." She smiled at me.

I thought about my adventure at Riverview. She was right. After volunteering one day at the luxury senior living facility, I'd taken a part-time job there assisting the activities director. At the same time, I aided one of the residents, Louise, in discovering what had happened to one of the nursing aides. I also figured out who was stealing from the residents.

I did help people. I even made a few friends along the way. My thoughts returned to last night. I remembered Lacy lying on the ground and screaming for help. I wondered if anyone would help her. I wondered how she was doing today.

"I wonder how Lacy is doing," I whispered across the table. My mother smiled sympathetically.

"I cannot believe the violence in this city. That poor woman." My mother wrinkled her nose in disgust. I recognized the familiar lament.

As long as I had known my mother, she had detested any form of violence. While she loved reading a mystery or thriller, she hated to witness anything remotely bloody. Even as children, my sister and I were forbidden from watching *Magnum P.I.* because there was too much shooting. In fact, when my sister and I would fight, my mother would sometimes splash us with water, separate us and then demand that we offer heartfelt apologies with a three point action plan for how we would resolve our problems in the future. Now that I thought about it, she probably should have helped negotiate peace in the Middle East. For my mom, there was always a better way than to resort to violence.

Before I could say anymore, the waitress approached the table for our order. My mother chatted with the waitress and asked her about her life before ordering oatmeal. I ordered the eggs, sunny side up, bacon, grits with cheese and toast. My mother raised an eyebrow.

"What?" I asked innocently. "Fear makes me hungry."

Chapter 4

We arrived back at the house about 10:30 a.m. My mother headed off to Latter Library to volunteer with the Friends of the Library. She would be sorting books. I wandered back to my bedroom and slipped off my shoes.

I shuffled into the kitchen in search of more coffee and almost had a heart attack seeing my Lucky dog costume lying over a chair at the kitchen table. I sat down next to the wiener and sipped my coffee. I thought about what I needed to do that day. Probably number one was return Lacy's phone, number two was return this costume and number three was find a good full-time position. I sunk into the chair.

Yep, I knew what I should do first. I should return this phone, but somehow I was inspired. I decided that I would heed my mother's advice. I would look through the jobs that I was originally applying for and only apply for ones where I thought that I would be helping people. I also looked through Craigslist for any non-profit listing. Surprisingly, I found two listings that seemed very promising. One was for an educational non-profit and the other was a listing for an Episcopal Church in Metairie that was looking for someone.

I had to laugh. Of all places, I found the small ad asking for someone who would lead outreach. Okay, I would actually send out a cover letter and resume to the church in Metairie. I hit the send button and felt good. I prepared the next cover letter and resume for the non-profit and with renewed purpose and energy I shot off the next resume and cover letter. I inwardly patted myself on the back.

Before I could start on another cover letter, my conscience started to nag me. Usually, I dragged my feet when it came to sending resumes, but not today. Today I was like a machine sending resumes. Yet, I knew the reason I was so motivated. Clearly I wanted to avoid seeing Lacy and thinking about the night before, but my conscience wanted me to do something.

What could I really do? I knew what hospital she was in, but I didn't know her last name. Would I be able to find her there once I got to the hospital? I stood up from the kitchen table and got dressed. I returned to the kitchen, again almost screaming when I saw the hotdog. Who knew a hotdog could be such a frightening reminder?

I sat down at the table again and looked up the local news on my computer. I would try to distract myself. I clicked on the nola.com website. I had avoided looking at any news last night, and I'm glad I did when I came across an article. The title was "Hooker and Hotdog attacked on Dauphine Street." Talk about click bait! My cheeks immediately flushed red.

If the article had not been about me, it would have been pretty hilarious. On the other hand, the writer made everything sound so salacious. The writer described the crime and took every opportunity to make some sort of hotdog/ sausage/frankfurter/ wiener pun imaginable. That part was pretty funny because I was dressed as a hotdog, but the part about Lacy was not funny. It implied she was a hooker and I was positive that Lacy was not a prostitute. She was just dressed that way for the movie. The article didn't even mention that part.

That was it. I had avoided it long enough. I needed to return her phone. I wracked my brain trying to remember where the ambulance was taking Lacy last night. I thought she had told me her name, but I couldn't remember it. Finally the idea hit me, I would call Jason.

Aaah, Jason Stone! Jason Stone was a police detective I'd met a few weeks ago at Riverview. Actually, a more accurate description of Jason was that he looked exactly like Jason Statham and he was a police detective who usually worked in the theft/robbery division of the NOPD, New Orleans Police Department. Admittedly, I really have developed a bit of a fixation on him, especially after discovering that he has a sense of humor and he should probably never wear shirts, but I digress.

I cleared my voice and dialed. He picked up on the second ring, "This is Stone." I immediately coughed into the phone and began to ramble.

"Uh, hi, Stone, I mean, Jason. This is Denise, Denise Stone, I mean Denise Reed. Definitely Reed." I died just a little bit inside. I heard a soft chuckle.

"Hello, Denise! How are you doing?" he asked. I was imagining him smiling. I think he must have been smiling. I may not have game, but I can make a man laugh.

"I'm good. How are you?" I wondered if he was wearing a shirt right now. I could see him jogging toward me in Audubon Park, no shirt, and nothing but lean muscle.

"Okay. What can I do for you?" He could always cut right to the chase. I tore my mind from imagining him without his shirt.

"Uh, yes. I'm trying to find someone. Last night, I was with a woman who got attacked on Dauphine Street. I'm trying to find her and return her phone. I don't know her last name." He became very quiet on his end. I wondered if we were disconnected.

"I know what you're talking about. You were there? What were you doing with her?" Jason asked. I could hear concern in his voice. I also noticed that he didn't answer my question.

"Yes, we were both extras in the Chase Clarke movie they were shooting in the French Quarter." I could almost imagine him shaking his head. I waited for a response.

"Unfortunately, I can't give you that information, Denise. Frankly, I kind of don't want to," he finally answered.

"Why not?" I asked. Why wouldn't he want to share this information with me? We were friends. He and I shared witty banter. I flirted with him. Of course, he usually laughed, thinking I was joking. I imagined him kissing me. He probably imagined me telling him good jokes and funny stories. Still, I could build a whole relationship around this in my head.

"You have a way of getting into trouble," he stated matter of factly. I wanted to argue with him, but maybe he was right. Who else could find herself flailing on the ground dressed as a hotdog next to someone who had been stabbed?

"What do I do with her phone?" I asked. I needed to do something with it.

"You probably should drop it off at the station, but I'm not sure who's heading that investigation. Look, sit tight and I'll call you back when I find out who that is. Okay? Bye." He hung up before I could even say goodbye.

I walked to the den and picked up her phone from the arm of the couch. I flipped it over in my hand. Which hospital did the paramedic say last night? I returned to the kitchen and my hotdog costume. If I could not return Lacy's phone just yet, maybe I'd go return the costume instead. At least I could put the indignity of being crushed under a celebrity, dressed as processed meat behind me. I closed the laptop and headed for the door.

Chapter 5

Driving to the French Quarter is terrible in New Orleans. I'm not sure if there is ever a good time to drive down there, but clearly I picked the wrong time. First of all, Uptown New Orleans was like driving through a labyrinth trying to avoid construction; parts of Nashville Avenue and even Jefferson Avenue were closed. The closer I got to the Central Business District it seemed like I got behind every delivery truck imaginable. When I finally made my way near Canal Street, I still needed to find a place to park. I ended up driving all the way to the New Orleans' Athletic Club and parking in their lot. Once I had pulled into the lot, I realized that I'd have to carry my costume almost four blocks through the French Quarter to get to the movie location. I remembered that the night before all the extras checked in at a trailer on Royal Street.

November can be a dry month in New Orleans or not. As luck would have it, as soon as I exited the garage and headed down the street, I noticed the first drop hit the pavement. While the hotdog costume wasn't that heavy because it was primarily made of some foam like material, foam can act like a sponge, especially when the sky decided to release its full contents on the three or four blocks that I was traveling.

I tried to move quickly, but the street was crowded and the costume was awkward. Bourbon Street was the usual tourist-filled street of debauchery, except today it was also soggy. There was no sign of a film crew. That didn't surprise me. Surely they needed to have it open to tourists during the day. I kept walking.

I finally made it to the corner of Royal and Iberville where all the trailers and movie equipment has been staged the night before. The street was empty except for the antique stores and the temporary "no parking" signs for filming. Of course, they were gone. That seemed about right.

The rain was really coming down now. I had managed to stay somewhat drier under the overhangs of a few buildings, but now I was really starting to get wet and so was the costume. I inwardly kicked myself for not trying to call first. For that matter, I'd probably need the name of the production company for that. First though, I needed to get out of the rain.

I pulled the costume closer and ran between puddles and overhangs, stopping and then going again. I made a little bit of progress, but the costume was already getting soggy and heavy. I heard someone behind me make a comment about soggy dogs. I turned quickly to give them a look but when I turned I managed to lose my grip on the costume and drop it into the gutter. I shook my head at the mess, when I heard a bell chime behind me.

I stood in front of a tiny, cramped antique store. In the doorway stood a large man with shaggy brown hair, a broad grin and white paint-stained overalls. He shook his head at me. "Let me help you out, sweetie!" He moved quickly past me and picked up the costume and walked into the store. I followed behind him.

"What is this crazy thing?" He flipped the costume over and began to chuckle. "Oh my, this is a hoot!" He carefully placed the costume on a wooden table behind his counter. I watched as he inspected it closer. He picked up a pair of glasses and put them on. He walked back and forth along the table, touching various parts of the hotdog.

"Thank you for helping me," I said quietly behind him. He finally stopped and faced me fully. He offered the fullest and friendliest smiles I have ever seen. Something about him was familiar, but I couldn't put my finger on it.

"I am sorry. I just took over. I saw you walk past here a few minutes ago and then when I saw you walking back and then, well, my name is Duncan Valmont." He wiped off his palm on his overalls and then extended his right hand. I took it gladly and shook. He immediately handed me a business card. The cream and gold embossed card announced the name of the store as Valmont Antiques and Gifts.

"My name is Denise Reed. It's nice to meet you, Mr. Valmont." He crinkled his nose at me.

"My father is Mr. Valmont. Call me, Duncan!" He smiled again. That is when I recognized Duncan! "Hey, where did you go to high school?"

Duncan puffed up and placed his hands on his hips, "Why, I went to De La Salle, graduated the year the girls came." He stuck out his tongue and laughed. "Wait a minute; we did a play together, didn't we? Wow! It has been a while."

I nodded and thought back to the high school musical and the gentleman in front of me. Going to an all girls' school, one remembered the boys who participated in our plays. I remembered his amazing voice and he always wore a bandana. He was so dramatic. I smiled at the memory.

"Do you still have that bandana?" I asked. We both laughed when he pointed to the bald spot on the back of his head.

"I graduated to fedoras! It has been such a long time!" Again we laughed. We spoke a little bit about the two plays we had both been in, what he did after he graduated and our families and friends in common. In New Orleans there are only three degrees of separation from any individual to another.

"Do you still do plays?" I wondered if perhaps he had stuck with acting. I remember him being an amazing singer and dancer.

"A couple of friends and I have started a little theater company. We aren't doing anything too complex. We do plays a couple of times a year at a small warehouse in Uptown. You should audition for the next show!" His eyes glowed as he described his theater company. I had to admit that it sounded fun.

I looked around the shop. The space was chaotic and comfortable at the same time. I could detect a slight scent of magnolia. At first I had thought it was just an antique or junk shop. One wall was filled with small knickknacks, souvenirs, and used items, but on the other wall was a jewelry case. I wandered over and looked down at the delicate pieces. Silver spirals and semi-precious stones sparkled under the glass.

"Did you make these?" I asked. The work was meticulous and beautiful. He beamed with pride. "Your shop is really cool. Thank you for letting me get in from the rain." We both smiled now. Then, as if something occurred to him, he tapped a finger to his lips. He turned and began rummaging in a cabinet behind the counter.

"I think you could use one of these." He pulled a huge black garbage bag from the cabinet and began to stuff the hotdog inside. "I just have to know. I know this is New Orleans, and this is the French Quarter, but what is with the hotdog costume?"

He continued with his stuffing and grabbed another bag. I just watched as he moved like a hummingbird and with such delicacy. I was mesmerized.

"Uh, well, I was looking for the movie company that was here last night. I needed to return my costume." I heard him answer a low, "uh huh."

"How fun! Did you meet any celebrities?" He turned around with an inquiring grin.

"As a matter of fact, I was knocked over by Chase Clarke!" I puffed up my chest and Duncan released a belly laugh at that.

"It's so fun when they have a movie shoot. I love that every single New Orleans-based film has an obligatory Bourbon Street Mardi Gras scene. Of course, the Quarter does make a great backdrop." He smiled at his statement. He was right. It seemed like every film did. "Everything is an outrageous New Orleans' stereotype, but then again, after what I see around here on a daily basis, those movies could be documentaries."

"I bet you must see a lot." He nodded at my statement. I'm not sure why, but at that moment I was curious. His shop was only a block away from where Lacy was attacked. Would he have seen what had happened? Would he know something?

"May I ask you a question?" I waited for Duncan to nod yes and then I continued, "Did you hear about that attack last night? It was just down the street."

He shifted his weight. He took a deep breath and stared back at me. "I heard about that last night. That just happened down the block." We both stood quiet in the store. "Some working girl and someone else got attacked. The police came by and asked me some questions this morning. They looked at the security tapes and all you can see is the girl walking past, a hotdog and maybe some tourists but you can't see anything else..." He stopped what he was doing and examined the hotdog costume before him. He looked at me with concern, "Why do you ask?"

"I was with that girl who was attacked. I fell over and couldn't really see anything," I answered. He clicked his tongue.

"That's scary. We've had some random crime down here, but you never know with those types." He crinkled his nose as if smelling something gross.

"What do you mean?" I asked. I wondered what he meant. Who were those types? I didn't understand what he was implying.

"I've lived in the Quarter my whole adult life. I love it, but it isn't Disney Land." He snorted at his reference. He was quiet for a moment and went on, "These streets are dangerous, but even more so for people in high risk jobs like that girl."

"Do you know her?" I leaned forward. He managed to smash the rest of the hotdog into the bags.

"I don't know her, but I know a dozen more like her. The police said she was a dancer and probably her pimp hurt her. I heard she works at Bad Daddy's and that place is notorious, if you know what I mean. And the police just turn a blind eye. It makes me so angry and sad. What were you doing with her?" He leaned back on the table and crossed his arms in front of him.

"We were in the movie together. I was just looking at pictures of her kid," I answered. He looked down.

"Oh, I didn't know. I hope she's okay." He spoke softly. He gingerly lifted the black bags and handed me my costume. He looked toward the front door of the shop. The rain had reduced to a drizzle.

"Thank you again. It was really nice meeting you again," I said as I took the costume and began walking toward the door.

"I am sorry. I guess I am a little strident in my views. That girl has a dangerous job, but I shouldn't judge her." He hung his head. I nodded in acknowledgment and walked out the door. As I wandered back to my car, I resolved that I needed to find out who had hurt Lacy and why.

Chapter 6

When I was back in my car, I headed toward
University Hospital on Canal Street. The facility was
huge. As I pulled in to park, I realized just how massive
the place was. How would I find Lacy there without her
last name? Still, I needed to try.

I made my way to an information desk. A large
white haired woman in a blue vest with a volunteer
badge sat in a swivel chair in front of a computer. She
chatted with an older gentleman wearing the same vest
and badge. I stood at the desk for about a minute while
the two ignored me and flirted. I coughed and then
smiled at her. She swiveled her chair and pushed her
glasses back on her face.

"Hi! I am trying to find someone. She came in last
night." I smiled broadly at the woman. She frowned at
me, or she just has resting grumpy face. I wasn't sure it
wasn't a mixture of both.

"A lot of people are in the hospital. Does she have a
name?" Wow! Loads of sarcasm for such a
grandmotherly type. I was not expecting that.

"You are right. There are a lot of people in this
hospital and she does have a name. Her name is Lacy."
The woman rolled her eyes at me.

"Does she have a last name?" She snorted this part. I
wondered why this woman had any business
volunteering at a hospital with an attitude that would
embarrass Oscar the Grouch.

"I don't know her last name, but she came in last
night." The woman just shook her head at me and

turned back toward the gentleman. I understand HIPAA rules. Certainly, I might not have Lacy's last name, but I was not going to be deterred in the face of such grumpiness. I wanted to grab the woman by that blue vest and shake her, but instead I decided on using a more subtle weapon.

"Ma'am, I really need your help. I may not know Lacy's last name, but I know that Lacy does have a last name. She has a name that someone who loved her gave her. She has a name that she shares with her daughter who is in first grade and in the Alpha Reading group. She has a name and is not just some statistic in your computer. I watched her get stabbed last night and I just pray she didn't succumb to her injuries." I laid it on thick. At this point, a crowd gathered around the information desk and the woman shrank in her chair.

"I can't help you unless I have a last name," she replied back quietly, as the crowd grew. I reached into my purse to retrieve the phone and pulled it out.

"What about a picture? I have been holding onto this since last night." I started scrolling through the pictures of Lacy with her daughter. The woman was turning an unflattering shade of red. The people surrounding the desk were murmuring.

"Hey, let me see that. I can find her last name." A short teenager with a tear in his t-shirt and basketball shorts took the phone from my hand, swiped and tapped a few time and handed the phone back to me. He'd found her name in her email! I hadn't even thought about looking there for her name. I turned the phone towards the woman behind the counter.

"She has a name." The young man spoke to the woman behind the counter and everyone became quiet. I smiled at him, as he wandered over to his seat in the waiting area.

She clicked on the keyboard and refused to make eye contact with me. She looked over at her companion behind the desk but he looked away. She whispered, "I think who you're looking for is on the fourth floor, room 438 East." I nodded down at the woman.

"Thank you," I said over my shoulder as I walked away.

I found the elevators and pressed the button. I entered the crowded car. It stopped on each floor, with a few folks exiting and entering. Finally it dinged for the fourth floor and I got off and looked for Lacy's room.

I stood outside her room and knocked. I could only hear a muffled sound so I pushed the heavy door open. Inside there was a curtain and I pushed it back. Lacy was sleeping soundly in her hospital bed. A monitor beeped next to her and an IV was attached to her arm. I moved a little closer to the bed and she stirred.

"Lacy?" I spoke softly and she seemed to struggle to open her eyes. She immediately shook herself awake and winced. The monitor let out a squeal. When she finally saw me, she let out a breath.

"Oh, it's you, Denise. How are you?" she asked weakly. She waved me closer and reached out her hand. I took her hand in mine.

I shook my head. "I'm doing fine. How are you?" She lifted her shoulders in a shrug. A tear started to form in the corner of her eye and then rolled down her cheek. I grabbed a tissue from the bedside table and handed it to her.

"The doctor said that it wasn't too deep. The knife missed hitting anything major, but I lost a lot of blood." She wiped the tear away and attempted to smile. She pressed her lips together, like she was stopping herself from telling me something.

"That was really scary last night. I've never been mugged before. What did that guy want?" I asked. Lacy bit the inside of her cheek and let out a breath. We were quiet for a moment.

"I have your phone." At that, her eyes grew wide. I pulled the phone from my purse.

She seemed to marvel at the iPhone. "It's not gone. That's good," she said almost to herself. I offered the phone to her, but she leaned away. She lifted her hand to stop me. "I don't think that would be a good idea. Would you hold onto it?"

"Don't you want it here with you so you can call people?" I asked. She shook her head. She hesitated, as if considering whether or not she could trust me.

"If you could just hold onto it for a few days while I'm here. I don't want to lose it. I was sure it was stolen and you never know in these hospitals. They say you shouldn't bring valuables here because they can disappear." As soon as she said that, she shivered. I wanted to ask her what she meant, but she interrupted me before I could speak, "Please hold on to it until I'm out of here."

"What about your family? Your little girl?" I tried to hand her the phone again. She pressed her lips together. I knew she wanted to tell me something, but she wouldn't allow herself to.

"They know I'm here. Please." Her eyes pleaded with me. "If it's too much trouble, my friend Charlie can pick it up. She's coming by sometime this afternoon before her shift. I'll tell her to call you so you can give it to her." She looked at me with desperation. She was sweating. The monitor beeped again.

"Okay, I'll hold onto your phone until Charlie calls and I'll bring it to her." The flush on Lacy's face began to fade and she relaxed into her pillow. She smiled at me. I began to stand to leave, when her grip tightened on my hand.

"Would you stay until I fall asleep?" She almost whispered her question, like a small child. I sat back down near her. "I was thinking about what we were talking about last night, you know, about you not knowing what this time was for." I was blank for a moment and remembered what we'd spoken about. I, too, had pondered the meaning of this not-so-free time while I looked for a new position.

"I think that you were given this time to save me." Her words hit me like a two by four between the eyes. She continued: "If you hadn't been there, I think he would have killed me. You scared him away." I was silent at her words.

"I didn't really do anything, but roll around on the ground," I said awkwardly. She giggled and the monitor beeped.

"See, there you go. Maybe it was to make me laugh." She went on and coughed and winced. She shifted in the bed a little and held my hand. Finally she was quiet again.

Her eyes began to flutter and I knew she was about to fall asleep. I watched her a little longer until her eyes shut and she snored softly. I looked down at the phone in my hand and put it in my purse.

Chapter 7

That afternoon, after drying off, I perched myself in front of my computer at the kitchen table. I sent a few more resumes, but I mostly scanned the different news sites for more information about the attack. I read a few articles. I also looked up Bad Daddy's website. I recognized Lacy's picture on the site. Her hair was pulled into two pigtails; one eye was closed in a wink. The image was suggestive, to say the least.

"What are you looking at?" I almost shot straight up from my chair. My mother stood directly behind my chair, putting on her glasses to read over my shoulder. She slipped into the chair next to me. I immediately closed my laptop.

"Yes, Mom?" I asked. I shifted in my seat to look her in her eyes.

"I've been thinking about that girl today, Denise. Have you heard anything about her? How is she doing?" My mother looked at me expectantly. A wrinkle appeared between her brows. She really was concerned.

"I saw her at the hospital today. She looks okay, but I don't know what's going on," I answered. My mother raised one perfectly shaped brow at me.

"What do you mean, Denise? The poor girl was attacked by a mugger. You were almost attacked by that same mugger. Thank God for that Lucky Dog costume!" my mother said. That was one statement I never thought I'd ever hear anyone say in my lifetime.

I shook my head and opened my laptop. "That isn't what I mean. I'm not sure it was a random mugging, Mom. I think something else must be going on. I feel like maybe she knew who did this to her." My mother turned the laptop towards her and looked at the Bad Daddy's website. I clicked off the website and on a newspaper article instead.

My mother clicked back to the website and twisted her head to look at me. "Why are you looking at this?" She was shocked.

"Lacy's a dancer at that place. That's her picture." My mother squinted at the screen. She looked back at me.

"That's the same girl? You're sure?" My mother sat straighter in her chair. Again she leaned closer to the screen, wrinkling her brow in thought. "That is a scary place." I wanted to ask my mother how she would know that, but I let the comment pass. Again I clicked to the news article.

Mom silently read the article. She muffled a laugh as she read. She took off her glasses and looked at me.

"Well?" I waited expectantly.

"Well what? The article is a little distasteful, but it doesn't say your name, thank goodness! What do you want me to see?" my mother asked.

"If this was a simple mugging gone wrong, why didn't they even mention that in the article? For that matter, why didn't he take anything from her? Why did it seem like she knew him before he...you know?" I asked and stood up from the table. I stretched my arms above my head and sat back down and faced my mother.

"Well, they don't have to mention everything in these articles. It was a mugging. Why would you think it was anything more? Maybe she did know him, or maybe she didn't know him. Maybe it was a pimp? Or a drug deal gone south?" my mother asked. She took off her glasses and twirled them between her fingers. I shook my head. "Either way, she's alive. You saw her and I'm sure that was a comfort and you gave her back her phone. Now you can be done with it."

"Well..." I hesitated and my mother raised one eyebrow encouraging me to go on. "When I saw Lacy, she was really sad. She thought that the mugger got her phone, but when I went to give it to her, she wanted me to hold it for her. She was worried that it could get stolen in the hospital, so I'm holding it until her friend calls," I explained to my mother. She clicked her tongue.

"You still have her phone?" My mother pondered this piece of information. I stood up and walked to the other room to retrieve the phone from my purse. I handed it to her. "What does she want you to do with it?"

"I guess just hang onto it until her friend Charlie calls to pick it up," I answered, shrugging my shoulders. My mother pressed the phone's home button and the screen brightened.

"Why wouldn't she want her phone with her?" my mother asked. I had no answer. She pressed the top button and turned the phone off. She put it on the table and tapped it with her finger. Then, Mom picked the phone back up and clicked it on. She started scrolling through something. Her eyebrows rose.

"What is it?" I stood up and tried to look over her shoulder. She lifted the phone so that I could see a long list of recent calls. There looked to be about 25 calls from a blocked or private number all in a row over a few days. "What does that mean?"

"Well, maybe someone has been trying to get in touch with her. Look, they called her again and again, almost minutes apart for days," my mother replied.

"That cannot be a good sign." She put the phone back down on the table. The phone rang and we both jumped.

"Hello," I spoke into the phone. It felt a little strange next to my ear.

"Look, Lacy, you better get your butt in here, if you want to keep this job. Mr. Gicardo said that he doesn't care who your boyfriend is. He's pissed!" I listened to the caller on the other end. It was a breathless younger woman. I wondered why she was calling me on my phone, when I remembered I had picked up Lacy's phone, not my own.

"Uh, wait, this isn't Lacy. She's in the hospital. Are you a friend?" I asked. The caller coughed and cleared her throat.

"Oh, she's sick?" the caller asked suspiciously. I could imagine this woman tapping a foot, leaning against the wall. "Well, what's she got? Is it contagious?"

"Last night someone attacked her. She's in the hospital," I answered calmly. I heard her repeat my words to someone else. The two argued, but I couldn't understand them. I guess she must have been covering the phone with her hand.

"Who's this?" she asked. I could tell she wanted to say some expletive, but she restrained herself.

"I'm a friend of Lacy's. I'm holding her phone while she's in the hospital. Who is this? Is this Charlie?" I asked. The caller let out a long breath.

"No, I'm not Charlie. I cannot believe you would think I sound like her," she said in a huff. The caller immediately hung up.

I looked at my mother and we both shrugged. I looked back at the computer screen and this time my phone rang. I looked at the number and looked at my mother. I didn't recognize the number.

"Hello?" I answered.

"Hello, may I speak to Denise Reed? I'm Carolyn Daspit of The Education Tree Organization. I received your resume and cover letter. May I arrange an interview with you for some time this week?" The voice on the other end sounded so hopeful. I was filled with excitement.

"Okay!" I answered. I grabbed my mother's arm and nodded like an idiot. We arranged a time for later in the week, said goodbye and I hung up. I slapped my hand on the table. "Hot damn!"

My mother scowled at me. "Denise, your language! What was that about?" Despite her reprimand, she smiled brightly.

"I sent in my resume earlier today. I took your advice and looked for a place where I felt that I could be helpful, not just another church, and now I have an interview this week!" I was practically bouncing out of my chair.

My mother pointed at me. "See, I told you. Let's see if there's any fat-free ice cream left in the freezer!" My mother turned to the fridge and began the search. Everyone needs celebratory ice cream, even if it is fat-free.

Chapter 8

An hour later, once again, I was slowly making my
way downtown, creeping down St. Charles, circling Lee
Circle and following the streetcar tracks to Carondolet.
Charlie had called and asked me to bring the phone to
Bad Daddy's. The streets felt packed. People were
getting out of school. I muttered curse words under my
breath. As I sat in my car, my cellphone rang. I
immediately picked up.

"Hello!" I answered brightly, hoping for, actually,
I'm not sure what. I guess I was surprised someone was
actually calling me and it was not a telemarketer.
Maybe it was Jason Stone just checking on me. That
would be nice.

"Hello, is this Denise Reed? This is Rev. Kent, from
St. Basil's Church in Metairie." Definitely not Jason
Stone, but I wracked my brain. Who was this? "Do you
have a moment to talk?"

I was speechless for a moment. I remembered why
the name was so familiar. I'd sent a resume to St.
Basil's Church earlier in the day. The voice on the other
end was so friendly and engaging and was actually
from another job prospect!

"Uh, yes, I'm in my car, but I can talk!" I slammed
on my brakes as a car ahead of me swerved into my
lane. I mouthed an expletive. Rev. Kent was quiet on
the other end. Had he heard what I just said about the
other driver?

"Hmm... sounds kind of dangerous. I wanted to let
you know that I received your resume and cover letter

today, and I'd like to set up a time to meet with you. Would you be available on Monday at 11:30 a.m.?"

I stammered and replied, "Yes!" I needed to pull over. This was the first time in four months that I actually had any actual prospects and now today I had two. My heart was pumping with adrenalin.

"Oh, wonderful! I'm so glad that you applied for the position. I've heard a lot about you. I just spoke with Father Foucher, from St. Christopher's..." With the mention of my former's boss' name, my heart sank. I could not imagine Rev. Foucher saying anything that would be helpful. To him, I was sure I'd be painted as a colossal failure and fool. Rev. Kent did not elaborate, and now I was dying to know what he'd said about me. Rev. Kent continued, "I'm looking forward to meeting with you and learning all about what you did there at St. Christopher's Church and what you've been up to since."

"That would be great, just great, Rev. Kent," I answered cheerfully, but I was unsure. How would this interview go? Would I have to explain about losing my last position because I talked myself out of it? That would be embarrassing. What would I tell him about what I was doing now? I wasn't sure that being a Lucky Dog was an impressive use of my time.

Rev. Kent said his goodbyes and hung up. I finally made my way to the edge of the French Quarter and miraculously found a parking spot. My eyes began to well with tears and then I cried. I wasn't sure exactly how I felt. Finally, I had an interview. Perhaps someone might want to hire me full time. I sat back in my seat and wiped my eyes and sniffed.

I flipped down the visor and looked at my reflection. My head was crowned with small brown frizzy hairs despite being pulled back in a ponytail. My make-up was non-existent at this point. I peered a little closer.

Was that a whisker on my chin? Where were my tweezers?

I flipped up the visor. I guess I would be as presentable as I would ever be, especially walking into the Quarter, and entering a strip club. Earlier I'd spoken with Lacy's friend Charlie. The woman on the other end of the phone had sounded frantic and like she might brush her teeth with a Taser or possibly use a drug that might mimic being shocked with a Taser. We set our meeting place at Big Daddy's before her next shift there.

When I finally pulled myself together, I grabbed my purse and phones and exited the car. I weaved quickly through the tourists and traffic, dodging a mule-drawn carriage at one point, until I was on Bourbon Street. I began my journey down the sidewalk.

I looked into the windows of the small tourist traps filled with hats, assorted Mardi Gras mementos and overpriced shot glasses. I side-stepped the long line waiting to eat at Galatoire's. Some young woman was murdering a cat in the Cat's Meow or perhaps trying to sing a karaoke version of Katy Perry's "Firework." Really too early to be that drunk, but hey, it's Bourbon Street.

I glanced at my watch. Charlie told me that her shift began at 4 p.m. It was already 4:10, but I thought that maybe I could still catch her and hand over the phone. I walked faster down the street towards Esplanade Avenue.

This end of Bourbon Street was just beginning to fill up. While it was still daytime, it felt less safe. Somehow everyone looked tougher and pirate-like.

Finally, I stood in front of the notorious Bad Daddy's. The French Quarter building must have been an old store front, but someone had removed the large plate glass window and replaced it with wood or metal panels covered in framed posters of who I can only imagine were the entertainment inside. A mountain stuffed into a neon orange muscle shirt and jeans perched on top a stool at the front door, reading a paperback. I could see that he had some sort of official badge and a walkie-talkie attached to his belt. When I stepped closer, I realized what he was reading.

"How do you like De Mello? Isn't his writing interesting?" I asked the bouncer. I had only known one or two other people who read the devotional book. The bouncer immediately held the book to his chest and tucked it into the back of his pants. So much for starting a very interesting book club. I was just left to wonder how someone like him ended up reading a devotional book at the front door of a strip club.

"Can I help you?" He practically growled the words. He really didn't need to growl. He was already as intimidating as a hungry grizzly bear and his voice sounded scary low. I gulped and tried to gather all the confidence I could find.

"I'm looking for Charlie." I smiled so hard that my cheeks hurt. He leaned from his perch on the stool and opened the metal door besides him. I stepped inside the club unsure what to expect.

It took a few minutes for my eyes to adjust to the dark. I expected the place to smell like beer and vomit and somehow be sticky. To my relief or amazement, the club smelled like cigars and clove cigarettes and my feet did not stick to the floor. There was a stage with the expected stripper pole in the center of the room. A bar wrapped around one end of it. On one side of the room were red leather chairs and sofas with small black lacquer cocktail tables. On the other side of the room, lining the wall, were about ten or fifteen black curtained booths.

I scanned the room, looking for a waitress or bartender to ask for Charlie. Four or five patrons sat lazily in their leather seats, some looking down at their phones, glancing up occasionally to see if anyone was on stage. I must have arrived in the midst of a break. Techno music blared from unseen speakers.

I steadied myself and walked toward the back of the club, weaving through the tables and trying not to look at either the stage or the booths on the other side of the room. For the most part, they appeared empty (thank goodness), but I didn't want to know what happened behind those curtains. I found a hallway with a sign for the restrooms and the office. An emergency exit was at the very end of the hall.

There was actually a fifth door down the hallway with a star on the door. I figured this might be where performers put on their, uh, costumes? I stood right outside the door and hesitated. What was I doing? I shook my head. I would hand this phone to whoever Charlie was and walk away.

I knocked on the door, but I couldn't hear a reply. I knocked again and the door swung open. A woman in a pink terry cloth robe, a neon green and silver wig, and more glitter than skin held the door open. She leaned against the doorway and crossed her arms in front of her, revealing her red nails with rhinestones.

"Yes?" she asked in exasperation. The woman was in a hurry. I'm sure she had more glitter to apply to her body, but I just wasn't sure where because it looked like she had it covered.

"I'm looking for Charlie," I replied brightly. The woman rolled her eyes in disgust.

"She didn't show up for her shift. So she ain't working here no more." She said the last part while whirling her index finger in the air. The woman promptly closed the door in my face. I stumbled back, almost tripping and hitting the wall opposite the door.

I had only spoken with the woman an hour ago. She'd asked me to come to Bad Daddy's before her shift began. I knew I was a little late, but apparently strip clubs ran a tighter shift than the army. Charlie should have been there.

I started walking down the hallway and stopped in front of the door marked "Office." I wondered what might be behind the door. Maybe the woman in the dressing room was wrong. I knocked at the office door.

Before I could knock again, the door opened a small crack and then widened. The man who looked out appeared to be about 60, thinning dark hair and deeply tanned. His bright blue silk shirt stretched over his belly and the top of his black leather pants. The man who peered through the crack looked terrified. His eyes inspected my body, resting right on my chest. His untamed greying eyebrows rose as if he was inspecting a cut of meat. I suppose he was, but at last he made eye contact.

"What do you want?" He was abrupt and looked impatient. Apparently today would be the day of rude interactions.

"I'm looking for Charlie. I have to give her something." His eyes searched my face and looked down at my empty hands. He considered what I was saying.

"Why do you need to see Charlie?" he asked suspiciously. He opened the door a little wider, revealing a plain metal desk with a lap top, a black cushioned chair and a wall of monitors. The club must have been filled with cameras at every angle and in places one might not expect, like the curtained booths. "I run a clean place here. I don't have any time for druggies or dealers."

I blinked at his accusation. He threw his weight forward on one foot towards me. I teetered back a bit. He kept moving forward.

"Lacy wanted me to give her something," I quickly explained. Somehow I didn't feel totally comfortable sharing more with the gentleman. His expression softened when I mentioned Lacy's name. He leaned back again.

"How do you know Lacy?" He was genuinely curious.

"We were in a movie together and I was with her the other night when she was attacked," I answered. Again, he considered what I'd said. He scratched the side of his face, thinking about how to respond.

"Charlie didn't show up for her shift," he said matter of factly. He raised an eyebrow, like maybe this was not his first experience with someone not showing up for work.

"Have you called her? Is she okay?" He looked at me as if I was insane.

"Why would I call that crazy chick? She didn't show up for work. She's gone." He flared his nostrils in disgust. "What did Lacy want to give Charlie? Maybe whatever it is, you should give it to me." From his tone, I could tell he was skeptical. Perhaps he thought I was actually delivering drugs to Charlie. He stepped completely out of his office and into the hallway. I stepped back. The man filled the space. He moved closer to me.

I stepped back again and my back was against the opposite wall. He moved so that he blocked my path. He placed one hand on the wall, next to my head. The hair on the back of my neck stood up and heat rose in my cheeks. I thought this guy might clean my clock if I didn't get out of there. I also thought that perhaps I should not entrust Lacy's phone to this man.

He might not have been huge, but he was definitely bigger than me. Would I be able to push past him? If I didn't act quickly, I was sure he would get pretty physical with me. I pulled out one of my most effective weapons: rummaging in my purse.

"Okay, okay." I dug into my purse, purposely avoiding Lacy's phone. I pulled out a handful of paper napkins. "Gee whiz, where did I put it?" I handed him the paper napkins. Then I handed him a few crumpled receipts, a crushed cracker in plastic, a Chap Stick covered in hair, a pink plastic ring from the top of a cup cake. His hands were filling with items. I wondered when the last time was I'd cleaned out my purse. Finally, I found what I hoped would distract this thug until I could rush down the hall and out the emergency exit. I handed him a maxi pad.

He took it from me and then dropped all the items on the floor in disgust. He stepped back, giving me enough room to make a dash for the back door. I took my opening and ran, pushing the bar and heading into what must have been a tiny courtyard at some point. I could hear him shout behind me, but I was already to Bourbon Street and heading back to my car. I was unharmed and my purse was finally cleaned out.

Chapter 9

I returned to my car breathless and sweaty. I tossed my purse on the other seat and started the engine. I was about to put my car into drive when my cellphone rang.

"Hello?" I asked, unsure who would respond on the other end.

"Hi, Denise, it's Jason." Immediately the anxiety and adrenaline seeped out my toes. I sighed. "Are you okay? You sound kind of breathless," he said. I must always be breathless when it came to Jason Stone.

Detective Jason Stone was sex on a stick, as one of my friends used to describe her crush of the week. He was the spitting image of Jason Statham with probably three more inches and a slight New Orleans twang. He and I had become friends at Riverview, the retirement community, where I worked sometimes. He was actually a detective—undercover—who worked primarily in theft and burglary.

"I'm okay, just a little shaken. What can I do for you, Jason?" Perhaps the question should have been what wouldn't I do for him?

"What do you mean 'shaken'?" The man was a detective. He missed nothing.

"I maybe had a little altercation with someone. I think it's probably fine. What do you need?" I tried to change the subject.

"What do you mean by 'little altercation'?" Jason was like a dog with a bone. I heard him sigh, "Where are you right now?"

"I'm in my car," I answered truthfully.

"Where?" I hemmed and hawed. I didn't want to tell him, but somehow I couldn't keep anything from him. He looked just like Jason Statham. Who would keep anything from Jason Statham?

"I'm parked on the edge of the French Quarter. I was trying to return Lacy's phone," I mumbled.

"I want you to meet me at the Riverwalk food court. Can you be there in about 10 minutes?" I looked out my windshield. The traffic was really picking up in the Quarter, but I was on the edge of it. I could snake around and maybe get there in 10 minutes.

"Okay, I'll see you there." I slipped into traffic. Fifteen minutes later, I rolled into the parking lot in front of the Riverwalk. To my left was a magnificent mural of a whale. I swore under my breath about the cost of parking: $3 parking with a $20 purchase, unbelievable! I made my way to the escalators near the Convention Center and entered the mall along the Mississippi River.

The food court was busy. Children and exhausted parents were crushed into the small play area. Every food stand had long lines with confused convention goers trying to figure out the menus. I weaved my way through the lines and headed toward the tables that lined the windows. The view of the rolling river was magnificent. I guess it was worth the crowd and high prices to park.

"Over here, Denise!" I heard someone shout from the tables. I looked over and there he was. Jason waved at me from his chair. "I got you a drink." This day was turning around quite nicely. I smiled at him. I felt like I could only see him and he could only see me.

I made my way to the table. He looked up at me casually. He looked amazing with a little hint of five o'clock shadow. He was pulled together in a blue blazer and khaki slacks. If he had a tie, it was gone now. The man could make anything look cool.

His long legs stretched in front of him, as he rolled his shoulders. The simple movement reminded me of a leopard stalking through the jungle, if the leopard was sexy like Jason Statham. That's when I noticed the man right next to him. I guess we were not having a drink alone.

The man sitting next to him smiled sweetly at me. He could have been Jason's complete opposite. While Jason appeared relaxed, the man next to him sat with Marine-like posture. Jason's hair was just like Jason Statham's hair—non-existent. This man's hair was a full mop of brown curls. Jason was cool. This guy almost knocked over the table to stand up and greet me.

"Hello, my name is Brock. Are you Denise?" The stranger reached across the tipping table and shook my hand. Jason steadied the table as Brock gestured to a chair.

"Hello, Brock, my name is Denise. Nice to meet you," I answered. Brock reminded me of a curly-haired Brendan Frasier. He seemed cute, but kind of clumsy. He held onto my hand for a tad too long and he just stared. Jason looked up at him and grimaced. At last he finally let go.

I sank into the chair between the two men. Brock waited for me to sit down before he returned to his seat and posture. Jason just stared at his friend.

Before I could ask anything, Jason offered me a Styrofoam cup. I lifted it in a salute. I thought he'd handed me a daiquiri. Without looking, I immediately sucked down something lumpy, and I instantly regretted it. I'm not sure what it was, but it might have been the unfortunate love child between seaweed strained through a dirty gym sock and a banana. I attempted not to gag.

"Do you like it?" he asked brightly. "It's a kale smoothie. They're excellent for energy." I held my lips together tightly and nodded, forcing the liquid down. I could do this, if I just sipped slowly. Maybe I could knock the cup over, except for the stupid plastic top! If only I could drop it in my lap, maybe that would work?

"Those smoothies are terrible, Jason. Nobody likes them." Brock took the words right out of my mouth, but I wasn't going to say it. I glanced at the ceiling as if I was staring at the Sistine Chapel. I was not wading into this quagmire. Again I tried to suck down a little bit more. My eyes were watering.

"It's good for you," Jason answered. At that moment he sounded like a fourth grade health teacher. I noticed a bird perched in the metal rafters. Yep, fascinating.

"Whatever," Brock replied. He picked up his drink and sipped. I bet his didn't taste like Swamp Thing's bath water.

"Do you work with Jason?" I decided I'd change the subject. My stomach was in all out revolt as the liquid hit it. It might have been healthy, but try telling that to a 34-year-old French fries and gumbo loving gut! I put the smoothie down and directed my attention to Brock. He nodded and smiled. Something in his expression seemed expectant, like he was waiting for me to say or do something.

"I have to say that I'm glad to finally put a face to all those stories Jason was telling at the station about you." Somehow that did not sound like a compliment. "Jason said that you get into a lot of trouble. You're not at all what I expected from the way Jason described you." I blushed and stared at my lap. I wondered how Jason had described me.

"Brock," Jason sounded like he was correcting an over excited toddler. The two men exchanged some sort of message through eyebrows and nods.

"Sorry. You look lovely." Brock again smiled at me. Again, he stared for a little too long so I had to look away. I picked up the dreaded smoothie and swirled it in my hand, like that would make it any better at all.

The compliment took me by surprise, but I took it. "Thank you, Brock." I raised the smoothie in my hand as if to take another sip, but I just held it. I thought about Brock's words and contrasted them with what I thought Jason might have said. I frowned.

I turned to Jason, "You described me to people? Good Lord, what did you say?" I looked between the two men.

"Nothing. I just told them about the time at Riverview. That's all." He sipped his smoothie. I thought back to the time at the nursing home and meeting Jason. Whatever he'd told his friend, it certainly had made an impression, but I'm not sure it was a good impression. He was not going to say any more about it.

"Denise, you look a little ragged." At first I was indignant at the comment, and then I looked down. My jeans had dark streaks on them. I could feel my hair unraveling in the back. I reached up and felt something in my hair. Was it grass? How had I gotten grass in my hair? I subtly moved my hand and stared at him as I continued to down my drink all the while praying that my taste buds would just go numb from the trauma of the smoothie.

I silently squinted at him. Now it was Brock's turn to give Jason some silent nod and eyebrow communication. Jason straightened in his chair. "I mean, what happened?" I put the drink down on the table with force. Jason and Brock both sat up.

"Well, first I tried to return my stupid hotdog costume this morning, and the movie must have changed location. Then I tried to return Lacy's phone at the hospital, but she wouldn't take it. She asked me to give it to her friend. Her friend called and then when I went to drop it off at Bad Daddy's, she..." Jason stopped me right there.

"Wait! Did you say that you went to Bad Daddy's?" I could tell that Jason was imagining this in his mind. A grin crept across his face.

"What were you doing with a hotdog costume?" Brock asked. He was completely puzzled.

"You've been to Bad Daddy's?" I asked Jason innocently. I then turned to Brock. "I play a Lucky Dog in the latest Michael Murphy and Chase Clarke movie." I returned my gaze to Jason, waiting for a response. Jason raised an eyebrow at me and sat back in his chair. I wondered about just how much time he might have spent at Bad Daddy's or in what capacity. I didn't want to think about him hanging out in a place like that.

"What did you do while you were a hotdog?" Brock was perplexed. Jason curled his lip and just stared at his friend, again sending some sort of ESP message to his friend.

"Please continue," Jason said, motioning with his hand. He shifted slightly in his chair. He looked me in the eye. This was when I noticed that his pressed Oxford cloth shirt actually matched his eyes. How could one man look so good especially at the end of the day? I glanced over at Brock. He looked pretty good too, fit, maybe a little stiff, but his suit was wrinkled. What had his friend told him about me?

Shaking my head, I continued with my tale, "Turns out that Lacy's friend was not at Bad Daddy's. Instead I ran into who I guess was her boss who cornered me and wanted whatever I was supposed to give to Charlie." I let the last part out in a huff. I slumped back in my chair and looked down. At some point during the day, I must have wiped grease on my shirt. Yep, that sounded like something that would happen to me. Grease on the jeans, grease on the shirt, grass in my hair sitting next to GQ and Brock, the clueless wonder.

"That sounds like a rough day," Jason replied. I just looked at him, expecting him to elaborate. He took a slow sip from his drink. Brock excused himself from the table and went to find the little police officer's room. I watched as he walked away, not a bad view.

"So?" I finally asked. Why had he called me here? Did he want to share something with me? He looked at me with a blank expression. I went on, "Why did you want to meet?"

"Oh yeah. I found out who the officer on this case is. Her name is Detective Antoine. She said that she'd probably call you tomorrow and also she can come by and pick up the phone from you and return it to Lacy Phillips." He took another long sip from his drink.

"What?" I was so exasperated. He could have told me this over the phone. I thought about the lost hours spent trying to return the phone and the costume. I also thought about how expensive the parking at the Riverwalk was.

"Denise, I said you should sit tight earlier today," he answered and shook his head. I thought my head was about to explode. "I figured after your day, you might have needed a drink." He raised his cup in salute. Somehow I couldn't help but laugh.

"Did Detective Antoine tell you anything about the case? Who tried to hurt Lacy?" I went on. I sat up to listen to his response. He sipped his smoothie and smiled. I wondered what flavor he got, probably not banana sweat sock.

"She thought it might have something to do with where she works. Honestly, we'll probably never know," he answered honestly and sipped his drink. I pressed my lips together.

"Why would she think that?" I asked. People seemed way too dismissive of Lacy and what happened.

"You've been to where she works. It's a rough place. It makes sense." I frowned at Jason. He shifted uncomfortably in his chair. "Why are you looking at me like that, Denise?"

"Somebody stabbed Lacy. She might work somewhere creepy, but she didn't deserve to be attacked. How can anyone be sure it wasn't something else? We need to find out what happened so that person won't get away with it or do it again!" I put my smoothie down and pushed it away.

"I didn't mean it that way. I'm just saying that she works in a dangerous place. Detective Antoine will find out what happened. You need to stay out of this," he explained. His stare pierced me. I muttered an "okay," but maybe I'd just poke around a little bit. Hey, I had the time.

I scanned the room and saw Brock making his way back to the table. "What is with this guy? Why is he here? What did you tell him about me?"

"He's Brock. We work together. Today we rode together. He wanted to meet you after I told him what you did at Riverview," he answered automatically. Was he being purposely vague? I had the sneaking suspicion that he was possibly trying to set me up with this guy.

"Are you trying to set me up with him?" I asked. Now I was perplexed. Jason grimaced.

"No," he said with such disgust that I was a little hurt.

Brock made it back to the table. He was breathless. "I just got off the phone with the station. We have a lead!" With that, both men said their goodbyes. I waited until they both left the Riverwalk, tossed the rest of the abomination of a smoothie, bought a daiquiri to take home.

I made my way slowly down oak-lined St. Charles Avenue, following the curve to Carrollton Avenue. I was going to pick up Emily at St. Mary's School. At last the school came into focus, hidden behind a fence and more Oak Trees. I turned right down Zimple and left down Short Street and parked.

I found Emily playing on the smaller playground at the pre-school building. She chatted with her friend and zoomed down a small slide at a dangerous speed. At last she saw me, she barreled towards me and wrapped herself around me. Her gorgeous brown eyes looked up at me.

"I told my teacher that you were a hotdog yesterday!" she said with glee. I hugged her tighter. Somehow, holding Emily made everything better.

Chapter 10

That evening, after putting Emily to bed, I decided
that a nice warm bath was in order. I sat in the tub,
soaking in the warmth when I heard my phone ring. I
ignored it.

I closed my eyes and placed a washcloth over them.
Again I heard a ring, but this time it was from my
bedroom. It was Lacy's phone that was ringing. I
wondered if maybe it was Charlie, so I immediately
leapt from the tub and wrapped myself in a towel. I
almost made it to the phone, when it stopped ringing.

I stood, dripping in my room, when once again, the
phone rang. I picked up on the first ring.

"Hello?"

"Hello, Charlie?" The voice on the other end was
unsure and I recognized it as Lacy's voice.

"No, it's Denise. I wasn't able to give her your
phone," I answered.

"How come?" Lacy asked with frustration in her
voice.

"She never showed up at Bad Daddy's to pick it up,"
I told Lacy, leaving out the other parts.

"Oh, great! She flaked again. She was supposed to
pick me up tomorrow, but I hadn't heard from her." She
clucked her tongue and released a loud sigh. "Would
you pick me up from the hospital?"

"Uh." I wracked my brain for an excuse not to do it,
but I couldn't think of anything. I hemmed and hawed.

"I wouldn't ask if I had anybody else, but nobody is available," she went on. I could hear a little sniff on her end.

"What about your boyfriend?" I suggested. There was silence from the other end.

"No, he can't," she answered icily. My ears pricked up at her answer. She went on: "He said we should break up." Again she started to sniff on the other end, like she was holding back tears. This time she was louder. Soon there would be full on waterworks.

"Okay, Lacy. I'll pick you up tomorrow. What time?" We set the time for her pickup the next morning. I would meet her at the door of the hospital and drive her to her car in the Quarter.

I returned to the bathroom and continued to dry off. This time *my* phone rang. I looked down at the number. It was Jason Stone.

"Hello?" I was unsure. He never really called me. What did he want?

"Uh, this is Jason." For the first time since I'd met Jason Stone he actually sounded uncomfortable.

"Yes, I know, Jason. Everything okay?" He was quiet. This could not be good. Had someone died? Was he moving to Australia?

"Uh, yeah. Can I give Brock your number?" The last part he almost whispered.

"What? Why does he want my number?" I asked. Of course, as soon as I said that part I realized how clueless I sounded.

"He wants to ask you out," he said with a pout. Hmm…now that was interesting. "I didn't know if you were dating anyone. I figured no but I thought I'd ask you before I gave it to him," he rattled on. What did he mean he didn't think that I was dating? I felt indignant that I was curious. I wanted to ask him if *he* wanted to give Brock my number. Again he got quiet.

"Um, okay, I guess so. Is that okay?" I wasn't sure why I asked him. It sounded like I needed his permission.

"Whatever you want, I don't care." Jason answered quickly. He sounded bored or maybe he was pretending to be bored. His words still stung.

"Well, if it doesn't matter to you, then fine," I said angrily.

"Well, fine!" he retorted. I guess two could play at the not having a witty retort game.

"Okay, good night!" I stammered.

"Good night, Denise!" he barked and hung up. I shook my head. I needed to go to bed and leave this day behind. A smile crept across my face. Was Jason Stone feeling jealous over me? I pushed the thought away.

Certainly I had fantasized about the man since I'd first set eyes on him. For that matter, every woman with a pulse at Riverview was drooling over him. We did talk quite a bit. We'd had supper together thanks to Emily inviting us to have dinner with him. He'd even kissed me—on the forehead. He was gorgeous, but I hadn't really thought that he might think about me too. I hoped it, but I didn't hold my breath. Still, the exchange was strange.

Chapter 11

At 10:45 a.m., I picked Lacy up at the patient drop off at University Hospital. She painfully maneuvered into the front seat of my car and winced as she snapped on the seatbelt. She was dressed in a hospital gown and scrubs, her feet in slippers. As I pulled out into traffic on Canal Street, she asked me to drive into the French Quarter to retrieve her Toyota parked on Dauphine Street. We drove in silence while she looked out the window.

"How are you feeling today? Is it less painful?" I asked. Even though I couldn't see her face, I knew that she was crying in her seat. I could see her shoulders seize up with her sobs.

"What did the police say? Will they be able to find the guy?" I asked hopefully. She turned towards me. Her eyes were puffy and red.

She shook her head. "I didn't talk to them. They don't care and it's over, so what does it matter?" I was about to protest when she pointed to her car. I rolled straight into a space behind the Toyota in the Quarter. Amazingly, I didn't see a boot on her car.

As I parked, she shifted in her seat and looked at me. She bit her inner lip and wiped tears away with her sleeve. She then began to rummage through her purse for her keys, dumping some of its contents into her lap and the rest fell onto the floor of the car.

"This day stinks! I cannot believe I just did that!" Lacy exclaimed and then released a line of expletives.

Immediately she slapped a hand over her mouth and looked over at me, unsure what my reaction would be.

"It's okay. This does stink. Let me help you get your stuff together." I smiled at her and began picking up random lipsticks, eyeliner, pens and other items from the floor of my car. She finally found her keys and clutched them in her fist. I dropped her make-up into her purse and she held the handle of the door.

"Lacy, before you go, are you sure you're going to be okay?" I gently touched her arm. She bit the inside of her lip, trying to keep herself from crying. "I feel like maybe you aren't telling me everything."

"What do you mean?" Lacy swallowed and pushed her hair behind her ear.

I didn't want to push her too hard and make her shut down. "Why didn't you want your phone while you were at the hospital?" Her eyes cast downward.

"I've been getting some calls. They didn't call last night, did they?" She looked frightened.

"No," I answered and waited for her reply.

"Then I guess it's over. I'll be fine." Finally she looked up and through the windshield, avoiding eye contact, "Thanks a lot for the ride. Thanks also for being with me that night. I was really scared." She adjusted her purse again as she spoke. She swung the door open and exited the car. I watched her walk around her car, get in the driver's side, start the engine and drive away. I felt sad as she drove away. I wondered if I'd see her again.

I guess I would never know what really happened that evening, but I wanted to figure out why someone would hurt Lacy. I suppose I should have minded my own business and shouldn't have cared, but then I thought about how frail and sad she looked. Someone had injured her and threw her to the ground like she was trash. It wasn't right, but what could I do about it now?

As I sat, my cellphone rang. I looked down at it to ensure it was actually my phone. It was. I *had* returned Lacy's phone. The number was unfamiliar to me, a California number.

"Hello?" I answered anxiously.

"Hello, is this Denise?" the cheerful voice asked. The voice had an almost valley girl accent.

"Yes, this is Denise," I said and waited.

"Hi, Denise, this is Nancy with Golden Shores Productions. You were an extra in the new Chase Clarke film in production now. We were wondering if you were available this evening for a re-shoot on Bourbon Street, starting at 6 p.m.?" she asked.

"Yes. Should I bring the Hot Dog costume?" I asked. Seriously, my life had come to a point where I now asked if I should bring the hotdog costume.

"Uh, I guess so. Hold on, let me check." I heard her shout a question to someone else. Then she said, "Yes, go ahead and bring the costume. Ellis is back so he can wear it." She spoke as if I knew who Ellis was. Maybe I would actually meet the original occupant of the Lucky Dog with his skinny hips? I wondered what costume they'd have me wear instead.

"Okay, I'll see you this evening at 6 p.m." I thought about returning to the set. I didn't particularly feel like going out this evening, but $50 is $50.

I began to turn the key in the ignition, when my phone rang again. "Hello?"

"Hello, is this Denise Reed?" the caller asked.

"Yes." I waited for the caller's response.

"This is Detective Antoine. I'm assigned to your case. I'd really like to speak with you if you have a few minutes. Would you be able to come to the station and meet with me?" the detective asked earnestly. I looked down at my watch.

"Uh, okay, but which station?" I wondered how long it would take me to get there.

"I'm at the 8th District, on Royal Street." She sounded so hopeful.

"I'm actually in the French Quarter right now, only two blocks away. I'll just walk there now." I took my key out of the ignition. I got out of my car and started walking down Dauphine Street toward Conti and took a right.

I arrived at the 8th District in no time. The building was a beautiful French Quarter building that looked more like a villa than a police station. I pushed the doors open and walked to the busy front desk, asking to speak with Detective Antoine.

Detective Antoine was a curvy African American woman with a megawatt smile. Her curly hair was pulled back in a bun, revealing tiny diamond studs in her ears. Somehow she looked like she should be wearing a business suit, stepping out of a high powered board room instead of around an ordinary brown desk wearing her neat blue uniform.

She immediately shook my hand and led me to a quieter room. She motioned to a chair and actually sat next to me. Something was comforting about her.

"First of all, I want to thank you for coming here today to speak with me. I really need to ask you and Ms. Phillips some questions about the attack on Tuesday night." She smiled. I immediately felt at ease. I had a feeling she was really good at interviewing witnesses.

"Yes, I'm happy to help anyway I can," I answered. For the next hour, Detective Antoine and I spoke about the attack. I tried to recreate the night for her. She laughed at my description of getting knocked over by Chase Clarke.

I told her about walking with Lacy to her car to look at her phone. She stopped me there: "So, you walked with her down Dauphine Street to look at pictures on her phone?" I noticed a slight tone. She was suspicious.

"Yes, we were talking about our daughters. We had a break. She wanted a cigarette." The detective scribbled this down on her pad. She tapped her pen against her chin.

"Do you know where Ms. Phillips works? Do you know what she does for a living?" The detective leaned back in her chair and waited for my response. I crossed my arms. I had a bad feeling about where this interview was going.

"Yes. I understand that Ms. Phillips works as a dancer at Bad Daddy's," I answered. I pressed my lips together. I heard Detective Antoine mumble an "uh-huh."

"Ms. Reed, were you with her to buy drugs?" she asked me point blank. I blinked and immediately sat up straight.

"Dressed as a hotdog?" I asked incredulously. She waited for me to answer her question. "Absolutely not! I don't use drugs, nor was she selling me drugs. She was showing me a picture of her daughter who is about two or three years older than my daughter. We were talking and it was nice, and then I fell over and then she was arguing with someone and then she was on the ground." The words tumbled from my mouth as I replayed the moment.

"Why would someone like you be talking with someone like her?" the detective argued. I felt like I was struck. Hadn't I immediately judged Lacy once she told me what she did for a living? I had been full of assumptions before I'd started talking with her, listening to her.

"I don't know. We started talking about the movie, just making chit-chat. Then we both talked about what we did for a living. She told me that she was a dancer. I told her that I'd lost my job, and she was really kind. It even turns out that our daughters go to the same school, St. Mary's. Before I knew it, we were talking about our kids, working, life..." I tried to explain why, but I realized that Detective Antoine was looking at me as if I was crazy. I released a sigh. "I guess I sound kind of crazy."

Detective Antoine chewed on the inside of her lip. I could tell that she wanted to ask something more, but she decided against it. "Maybe not crazy, just a little lonely," she almost whispered when she spoke.

"Do you know with whom she argued? Did she appear to know her attacker?" Detective Antoine suddenly shifted from your friendly neighborhood Officer Friendly to a Law and Order detective in a blink of an eye.

"I'm not sure. I couldn't hear them very well, but they argued. I assumed that the mugger was trying to take her purse or something and she wouldn't let it go," I speculated and then I closed my mouth. Detective Antoine lifted her chin. Her eyes inspected my face, as if she was trying to determine if I was telling the truth.

I let out a sigh and she leaned closer to me. "As far as we can tell, nothing was stolen from Ms. Phillips. Do you know any reason why someone might want to hurt her?"

"I have no idea. Like I said, I only met her that evening on the movie shoot." I shrugged my shoulders. "Have you spoken with Lacy?"

"She hasn't returned my phone calls," she answered dully.

"So, what will happen next? Do you have a suspect?" I asked anxiously. Detective Antoine stood up from her chair and stretched. She looked at me with pity.

"Nothing will happen if Ms. Phillips doesn't cooperate. She won't tell us what happened." She shook her head in disgust. With that, she thanked me for my help and escorted me to the front door of the station, handing me her card.

"Look, you seem like a nice lady. Maybe you can get your friend to speak with me. Please have her call me." I took her card and shook my head.

"I'll try," I answered, unsure if I would ever actually see Lacy again.

Chapter 12

While walking out the front door of the station, I felt unsettled after my interview with Detective Antoine. I've always been a believer in talking to the police. You should report crimes, but after my encounter with her I felt unsure.

Somehow I couldn't blame Lacy for clamming up. Speaking with the detective, I felt as if she was accusing me of something, and I was just a witness. Why would Lacy talk to the police if the first thing they thought was that she was selling drug, buying drugs or doing something else illegal? I decided I'd call Jason.

He picked up on the first ring, "Hey, Denise, how's it going?" He sounded a little breathless.

"Did I catch you right in the middle of something?" I asked. I could hear thuds and shouts in the background.

"Just arresting someone who's been stealing UPS packages off people's front porches. Did this in his own neighborhood, pretty stupid." I could hear him remind his suspect to bend down so he wouldn't hit his head. "What's going on?"

"I just finished meeting with Detective Antoine." I started and paused.

"Yeah, how did that go?" He listened.

"She made me feel like I was some drug fiend or maybe a suspect. Do the police think this is some sort of drug thing? I wasn't buying drugs!" I insisted furiously.

"No, these are some standard questions. Often crimes in the Quarter are drug or sex-related. I'm sure no one would ever think that you use drugs or buy drugs. You're too innocent," he answered. I was relieved, but also I was a tad insulted. He thought I was some goody two shoes?

"I just thought it was pretty bad. I guess Lacy won't really cooperate," I said. I let out a sigh, looking around Royal Street. Right now everything looked quaint, not seedy and dangerous.

"Then I guess that's that. You're finished with it," Jason answered. He sounded a little too enthusiastic.

"I am, but what about finding this guy? Will they find him?" I asked desperately. Someone else could be in danger.

"Maybe yes or maybe no. Either way, it isn't your problem anymore. So, did Brock call you?" Jason asked the last part with a mocking tone.

"Well, what if he did?" I replied. I heard Jason snort and then some juggling with the phone.

"I gotta go! Talk to you later." With that, Jason hung up. My mouth dropped open. Was that it? I wanted to smash my phone on the ground.

I slowly returned to my car on Dauphine Street. I was disappointed. Would the police capture Lacy's attacker? Why was Jason acting so weird? My eyes lifted from the sidewalk, up the building along the way. The architecture really was quite interesting in the Quarter with its amazingly intricate wrought iron and old brick. I wondered how many times I'd probably walked along this street in my life and never really checked out the beauty around me.

I stopped and my phone rang. I picked up before I even checked and knew that was a mistake. I heard the telltale cough.

"Hello, Denise, it's Father Foucher. Have I caught you at a bad time?" The question sounded sincere, but I could not help but feel my irritation rise.

Since I'd lost my position at Rev. Foucher's church, I had probably spoken to him about three or four times. Each time felt uncomfortable. Somehow I imagined him inwardly shaking his head in disgust. He had a way of looking at you that without words conveyed that he thought you were probably dumb as a sack of hammers.

"Yes, Rev. Foucher. I was just admiring some architecture in the French Quarter," I answered honestly. I was suddenly struck with how quickly my mood could change or how I could *let* my mood change. First, I was down about Lacy, but when I started looking around, enjoying the scenery I felt better and now I was letting a phone call with someone I found unpleasant dictate how I should feel. Hmm...

"You are blessed that you have the time for something like that. It's so important to be present in this world and appreciate the beauty. I love architecture, but working keeps me so busy." I rolled my eyes, grateful he could not see my response.

"I had no idea that you enjoyed architecture, Rev. Foucher." I idly chatted with him, waiting for what he wanted. I thought for sure he would get to the point, but his response surprised me.

"Actually, I studied art in college. I had almost enough credits for a minor in it. I wasn't that good, but it was so much fun. You know, you should go look at the scroll work at the Pontalba Apartments on Jackson Square!" Now I was shocked. In the years that I'd worked for the man and in the time since, I'd never heard him utter an unscripted or uncontrolled word. He would reveal nothing and had a façade of perfected pastoral professionalism mixed with a side of snob. For the first time, he actually seemed like a normal person.

"Oh, that's a wonderful idea. I think that I might do that," was all I could muster up to say. We were silent for a moment. Since I'd lost the position at the church I felt nothing but angry with Rev. Foucher, but for some reason, at this moment, I wondered if I ever really knew this person. Maybe he wasn't a pretentious jerk face?

"I'm calling to let you know that I spoke with Rev. Kent from St. Basil's Church in Metairie," I heard his dismissive tone when he said "Metairie." Nope, still pretentious, but perhaps he had some redeemable qualities. "It's a sweet place, no endowment really. The congregation, of course, is so much smaller than St. Christopher's. I'm not sure if you know the area, but it isn't a historic building or anything special." Hmm... maybe those redeemable qualities are really, really well hidden. "I did tell him what you did while you were here and that you left somewhat unceremoniously, but I'm sure that Rev. Kent won't hold that against you." Nope, definitely not seeing any redeemable qualities.

I squeezed my eyes shut. "Thank you for letting me know. Have a good day, Rev. Foucher." I wondered if he'd just torpedoed my chances with St. Basil's. It certainly sounded like it. This day was just getting better.

I looked down at my watch. I needed to get out of the Quarter before the area really became congested. "I better go, Rev. Foucher. Goodbye," I said.

"Enjoy the architecture, Denise. God bless!" He chimed as he dismissed me. I looked up at the buildings again. I would enjoy them as I strolled to my car. I might as well because I didn't have anything else going on at the moment.

Chapter 13

I arrived on the set at 5:45 a.m., with the hotdog costume in tow. While I was driving to the set, I'd noticed how much the costume stunk in my back seat. The smell was something between an old gym shoe and a dog that had rolled in dead squirrel. I would have to get my car detailed to get the smell out.

I looked around the set for someone in charge or someone I recognized from the night two days before. At last I caught a glimpse of Claudia. Her phone was pressed against her ear. She angrily spoke into the phone and then hung up. She marched right up to me and stood, tapping a toe at me. She turned her head to one side as she toyed with her shell necklace.

"Where have you been? It's almost call time. Also, you totally disappeared on Tuesday. I thought you took off with our Lucky Dog costume!" She looked at me, demanding some sort of explanation. Frankly, I'm not that fond of insistent toe tapping, unless it's tap dancing in a musical number.

"Someone attacked my friend with a knife. Here's your costume!" I held the stinky wiener out at her, urging her to take it from my hands. Instead she stood up straighter and stepped back, cleared her throat and gripped her necklace even tighter. Her nose twitched when she caught a whiff. We were both quiet for a moment.

"I guess the Quarter is a dangerous place for some people," she said blankly. I wanted to roll my eyes or slap her face. What a brainless thing to say? Instead, I nodded. She stepped back again, as if I might sneeze on her and she'd catch something. Then she turned on her heels and stomped off without another word. I stood there with the costume still in hand.

While I stood there, I heard someone with a bullhorn make an announcement. I couldn't make out what the person was saying. I noticed some other folks lining up and I followed the crowd. The gentleman ahead of me explained that we were getting our costume assignments.

At last I made it to the front of the line, lugging the hotdog costume. The woman looked down at her clipboard and then asked: "What's that?" She gestured at the costume with her pen.

"A Lucky Dog." I lifted it higher so she could inspect it. She scratched her chin with her pen and then tapped it on the clipboard. She waved a hand in front of her nose.

"Is this your costume?" she asked suspiciously. She used her pen to lift up one side of the costume and inspect it.

"I wore this costume last Tuesday night. The regular hot dog wasn't available," I answered dryly. I heard a few people behind me snicker.

"Oh, as it turns out, Ellis will not be here this evening either. He definitely has mono, so, would you be interested in being our Lucky Dog again tonight? We'll give you an extra $80." She waited for my answer, blinking expectantly. I sighed. I suppose being a hot dog was my cinematic destiny.

"Sure, why not," I answered unenthusiastically. The woman with the clipboard pointed in the direction of some trailers where I'd be greeted by the hotdog handlers to help me back into the costume.

The two handlers shoehorned me into the stinky costume. When it was finally on, I found a mirror and actually looked at myself. The costume had suffered a few scrapes and was a little dirty, but for the most part the foam had held up. I looked ridiculous, but I hated to admit that it was pretty funny and this probably would end up written in my memoirs or as a session with a therapist.

I toddled out from behind the trailers and made my way to where I'd been before on Bourbon Street. It was not as quiet this evening, probably because they could barely keep people off the street. I could hear tourists and drunks catcall and shout from behind some barricades as they watched all the extras assemble for the scene.

I looked for the duct tape "X" or maybe a glimpse of Chase Clarke, but I didn't see either. I scanned the group of extras, hoping that I might see a familiar face. I felt sad thinking that probably Lacy was not there and shook my head wondering about who her boyfriend was on the set. What a louse!

"Okay, everyone, we're going to be filming some different angles this evening. We want to get a few crowd shots. Let's just try to have fun with this," the elfin director announced to the gathered group. He pursed his lips and almost rolled his eyes on the last comment. His eyes fixed on me. Uh-oh.

He pushed his way through the crowd and again he stood before me. Immediately, Claudia ran up beside him. First he turned to her and just looked into her eyes, like he was psychically telling her to go grab him a coffee. She scurried quickly to the snack table. Then he stepped a little too close to me. I think he caught a whiff of the costume and stepped back.

"Let's not have any improvising this evening, okay?" He said it with a smirk. He gestured around to the crowd, as if inviting their laughter.

"Okay," I answered and turned. I noticed that the crowd of extras had shrunk away. I turned back and realized that he was still standing there. Now he was glaring at me. Ooh, an angry elf! "Is that it?" I asked.

At that, his nostrils flared. There was a collective gasp from the group. I could be wrong, but I think I was rubbing this guy the wrong way. Claudia snuck right next to him and gently tapped his shoulder. "What?" he asked with total exasperation.

"I have your coffee, Mr. Murphy," she whispered. She looked like he'd struck her, but when he turned towards her, his expression immediately softened. She offered him his coffee and he silently took the coffee from her and sipped, just staring into her eyes. He gently caressed her fingers.

I could barely keep my eyes from bulging out of my head. Come on, folks, let's keep this shoot PG! They were wrapped up in each other. I shifted around to see if anyone else was witnessing this little love fest. Everyone else seemed to be completely engrossed in chatting with other folks around them or inspecting the concrete on the ground. He actually pinched her bottom and she giggled. I sighed loudly, hoping that would bring the lovebirds back to reality. It sort of felt like I was intruding on something personal, but we were in the middle of a crowd. Claudia turned and looked at me with contempt.

She leaned toward the director and whispered something into his ear. His expression looked shocked and he shook his head. "Later. We need to talk about this later. It's fine. Let's just talk later, okay?" He looked back at me and forced a painful smile on his face. I smiled back. Somehow, I still think I was driving this man crazy. At least I was going to get paid. I really needed to get a real job. God, I hoped that my interview tomorrow or Monday would go well. I was pretty sure I would not have to dress as a hotdog at either place. Maybe at St. Basil's. I'd heard some fun stories about that church. At least I hoped I wouldn't have to ever dress as a hotdog again.

The scene began and again I was flailing around in my Lucky Dog costume and giving it my all. The shoot seemed to go on for hours as they would stop the group, move the camera, or adjust a light. After what must have been two hours, we had a break. This time I realized that I had no one to help me get a snack from the table.

I wandered near one of the barricades. Again, I could hear crude remarks about hotdogs. I scanned the crowd and heard a familiar laugh. Where had that come from?

"Hey, hotdog lady!" Finally my eyes landed on Jason. He made his way to the edge of the barricade. I wandered over to him.

"Hey, Jason! What are you doing down here?" I asked breathlessly. This costume really took it out of me. Yes, I was breathless because of the costume, not his amazing eyes, rock hard body, and throaty manly laugh. His gaze travelled up and down my body.

"I had to see this for myself. I heard they were shooting down here, so I thought I'd take a look." He raised a brow at me. I twirled around in front of him. "I am not disappointed." We both chuckled.

I heard someone say his name behind him. He turned around and raised one hand. He turned back to me. "I wanted to talk to you about something." I leaned a little closer to the barricade where he was. He waved me nearer.

Once again, I leaned too far and fell forward into his arms. My face fell flat onto a solid wall of muscle that was his chest. As annoyed as I was to fall, I have to say this time it wasn't so bad.

Jason righted me, holding my arms in a strong grip. I smiled at him. He rolled his eyes. Someone behind him said, "Say cheese!" I saw a flash. Jason turned toward the offender and scowled.

"I have to go, Denise. Good luck, Lucky Dog!" With that, he took off after his friend, the photographer.

I toddled back to the snack table and looked longingly at the bags of chips. I wandered around the set a little bit, making conversation with some of the other extras. I meandered over to where the cameras were and the lights, careful not to trip on any cords. Two or three crew members were fiddling with the back of one of the lights and talking.

"We freakin' had the shot two hours ago. This jerk is ridiculous," I overheard one man say to the other. I'm not usually one who eavesdrops, but I didn't have anything else to do.

"You know that we're over budget, right? The big guns are coming down this week. If he doesn't pull it together, they might pull the plug and my check better not bounce. We should have been finished a week ago. Perfectionist, yeah, right! He just likes spending his wife's money." That caught my attention. Were they talking about the director? Surely they were talking about him.

Now, I know one shouldn't gossip, nor listen to gossip, but when one is dressed as a hotdog and has nothing better to do, well, can overhearing gossip really be that bad?

"I'm ready to be finished. This movie is cursed, I tell you. First Colleen falling off the back of the trailer, then someone breaking into Lois' car, and then that other chick..." Before I could hear anymore, the two men stopped as their walkie-talkies crackled with static. Interesting, the movie did sound pretty unlucky for its crew.

I wanted to hear more, but the guilt was getting to me. Maybe I could seamlessly move into the conversation. I walked right next to the men and smiled. The two stopped talking immediately.

"Hi, I'm sorry to bother you two, but I have something in back of this costume that's itching me. Would you mind?" I waved my hand up and down, attempting to point to my back. One laughed at my gesture.

"Sure, turn around." I turned around and started directing him in adjusting the back of the costume. "Hmm... seems like it should be fine. I don't feel anything poking and it's in place."

I turned around. "Are you sure?" I asked innocently. My eyes scanned the light behind them, "Wow! What's that thing? What do you guys do?"

"We arrange and operate the lighting." They began to turn away from me, back to work. I needed to keep them talking.

"So, how does it look? How long have you been working on this film?" I asked cheerfully. One man sighed and went to grab coffee, but one decided to talk.

"It looks fine. We have been working on this movie for a year, but usually we only work about 10-14 months, at least my particular part. We're usually almost finished by now." He flipped some switch on the machine and adjusted it slightly.

"Why does it take so long?" I asked.

"This director hasn't had a hit movie in probably ten years," he grumbled, flipping another switch and looking back at me. "You aren't a reporter, are you?"

I shook my head as vigorously as I could.

"The break's almost over. I have to get this set up." With that, I was dismissed.

I heard an announcement that we should all be in our places and I walked back to my spot for the next bit of filming. We continued with this another hour or two. When they finally announced that it was a wrap for the evening, I almost shouted with joy.

Again, the director approached me. This time, I waited for the crowd to move away. "I don't know why I am telling you this, but I'm a very particular man. I like things a certain way and I get my way."

"Uh huh," I answered and waited. He pressed his lips together with frustration.

He took a deep breath and continued: "I don't like improvisation, and loathe as I am to admit it, I will need another shot with you in the Lucky Dog costume tomorrow. You will be at Café Du Monde at 5:45 a.m." He began to turn on his heel.

"Wait, I'm not available tomorrow. I have a meeting at 8:45 a.m. Can't you find someone else?" The next morning I had my interview with the Education Tree Organization. I was not going to miss an actual prospective job opportunity to dress up like a hotdog. He froze in his fancy brown leather shoes and turned around.

"Are you actually telling me 'no'? No one tells me no. I need my shot." He walked right into my personal space.

"Well, I am telling you 'no.' I have an appointment at 8:45 a.m. tomorrow. It's important." I tried to put my gloved hands on my hips. I could not reach. I dropped them by my side. He stepped even closer.

I tried to stand my ground. I knew I shouldn't really be that intimidated, but he looked pretty angry. I stepped back and began to trip over a cord. I instinctively reached out and grabbed his upper arm pulling him down to the ground with me. He let out a high pitched yelp, something similar in sound to what little dogs make when they're excited.

The others who had been walking away before, now turned around and looked at the spectacle. The director laid sprawled out on the ground right next to me. He turned and whispered: "You did that on purpose. I know that you did!" I let out a belly laugh.

"Look, you crowded me and I tripped over the wires. It was an accident," I answered as two members of the crew walked over and helped me up. I noticed that they were trying to hide their snickers. I also noticed that no one tried to help him up. Apparently so did he as he scrambled up and stomped a foot.

"Fine! You'll be here tomorrow at 10 a.m., ready in costume!" He stalked away. I watched him go and found myself laughing about the situation.

"What's so funny?" I turned to find Claudia right next to me. She startled me. One problem with this costume, among everything that was wrong with this costume, was I could never hear anyone approaching me.

"Oh, nothing really," I answered. It was too hard to explain. She cocked her head to one side and looked at me.

"You really get under his skin," Claudia said it wistfully. "I wish…" She stopped at that point, as if she realized that she'd spoken aloud.

"You wish what?" I asked. She was looking longingly as the director walked away. Ah, someone had a crush.

She totally ignored my question and continued: "Okay, then, tomorrow you need to be at Café du Monde at 10 a.m. with your costume. You might want to Febreze it or something, okay?" She patted me on the back and walked away.

That evening when I arrived home I thought about what the two crewmen had been talking about. I opened my laptop and typed in Michael Murphy's name.

Articles popped up about many of his latest flops. Others mentioned that he was having a hard time getting the money together to make a film.

I added Chase Clarke to the search and found an article about the current film. The article was a complete puff piece with one tiny mention about funding coming from the Quinn Group. I found a second article that implied that the picture was having many holdups, including some accidents on the set. The production seemed to have difficulty replacing those members of the crew. I looked for anything else and then I saw it, a grainy shot of a hotdog in what looked like the strong embrace of one police detective. The article mused: "Is Jason Statham making a cameo and a romance with a hotdog in Michael Murphy's newest film?" I decided I should probably go to bed at that point and hide under the covers.

Chapter 14

The next morning, after taking Emily to pre-school, I raced back to the house to change. While driving, I realized just how stinky my car was from the Lucky Dog costume. I needed to clean out the car; maybe a little vacuuming would help. I would go to the car wash that afternoon, after my interview and the filming.

I arrived at The Educational Tree Organization at 8:40, parking in the lot beside the red brick building on Camp Street and Girod Street in the Central Business District. The building was an old warehouse that now was separated into many offices. I entered the building, scanned the directory and tapped the button for the elevator to the third floor.

The doors dinged and opened, revealing a hive of activity. I stepped into the open floor filled with a noisy bullpen. In one corner, I spied a ping pong table. Some people were seated at desks chattering into headsets. It looked more like the common room of a dorm than an office. A young man walked past wearing pajama bottoms. I looked down at my grey suit. I was overdressed.

"You must be Denise! I looked you up on Facebook. I'm Carolyn's assistant, Kelly." A young red-haired woman wearing what can only be described as a romper approached me. She looked like she was about fourteen. Still, she seemed pretty friendly.

"Yes, I'm Denise," I answered. I found myself almost shouting. The room was noisy. She gestured for me to follow. She led me across the bullpen to a conference room, enclosed in glass. The logo of the organization—an apple tree—was emblazoned on the glass.

As soon as we entered the room and she closed the door, there was silence. I could not believe how quiet the place was. I saw a chair with a bottle of water on a coaster waiting.

"Please have a seat! Carolyn will be right with you." She pointed at the chair with the water in front of it. I sat down and smiled at Kelly. She opened the door and the room filled with noise until the door shut behind her.

I peeked at my watch. It was almost 9 a.m.. I was supposed to be at the movie shoot. I pushed it from my mind. I needed to focus on this interview. A few minutes later, Kelly returned with a blond woman, presumably Carolyn. She, too, looked about 14, wearing mile-high heels and a micro mini skirt.

I stood up and greeted the woman as she entered, reaching my hand out to shake her hand. The woman looked at my hand and cocked her head to one side. She leaned a little forward, again, examining my hand.

"Wow! Such formality, way old school!" the woman said perplexed and looked up at me. She reminded me of an emu, especially the way she moved her head. I tried not to be distracted by it. Still, she didn't shake my hand. Instead, she and Kelly sat down across from me, their backs to the bullpen. "My name is Carolyn. This is Kelly, my assistant. We will be conducting your interview, okay?"

The interview started with the standard questions. Carolyn asked all the questions, while Kelly stared down at her tablet in her lap and tapped away. I assumed she was taking notes or playing Candy Crush. She asked me about what outreach organizations I was familiar with, if I understood the educational needs of our area, and my familiarity with technology in education.

The questions were shot out in rapid fire succession and I tried to keep up. I answered them pretty well. It appeared that Carolyn was not listening to my answers until she asked what experience I had with children.

"I led a youth group of about 10 to 15 kids. I also tutored regularly with the STAIR organization," I answered quickly, ready for the next question.

"Wait, what?" Carolyn again turned her head like an emu.

"I tutored with STAIR. It tutors children in first and second grade with their reading," I answered.

"I know what STAIR is, but what is youth group?" she asked, this time turning her head in the other direction. Kelly stopped her tapping and looked at me as well, mimicking the same expression.

"The church that I worked for had meetings for kids where we would learn a little something, play games, eat food. That's youth group." Carolyn leaned forward and put down a pen.

"Wow! So retro! Who knew anyone did stuff like that anymore? Am I right?" She turned to Kelly for confirmation and Kelly vigorously shook her head. "I'm just going to say it. I feel like you bring such wisdom and depth, something the older generation has to offer."

I blinked for a moment. Was she talking about me? She thought I was old? She continued: "We tend to have a lot of turnover here. Lots of folks get really stressed out and don't know how to make that work-life balance. We could use someone who's, well, grandmotherly." Both women now looked at me and nodded.

I left the remark right there. "What would I be doing?" I asked. While I was initially hopeful about the position, I was getting the feeling that maybe dressing as a hotdog had its advantages.

"The large part of what we do is fundraising. While we focus here on the type of small scale gifts, we need to reach that market with deeper pockets: middle age. Someone like you could relate to their lives and struggles. You can figure out how and why they give, when there are so many choices for giving out there," Carolyn answered confidently.

"So, what does the Education Tree actually do day to day? Would I be working with children? Is it policy-making? I only ask because I know when approaching people about money they like to know what you do." I smiled at the two women.

Carolyn nodded vigorously. "You so get it! Yes, actually day to day we provide schools with online resources for students at home. The software interacts with the kids, so we don't need to," she explained.

"And you provide this free of charge to the schools and families I assume. That's why you need to fundraise?" I asked.

"Oh, no! It costs about $400 a classroom and for individual parents about $150. The fundraising is for continuing research into the best practices for teaching children online." I held the grin on my face, but I wanted to crawl under the table. This was just a tech company disguised as a non-profit.

"What about schools that cannot afford it? Or parents who don't have a computer at home?" The two women looked at each other and again I got the emu stare. "Does it follow the curriculum at the school?" I pressed.

Carolyn and Kelly leaned back in their chairs. Clearly no one had ever mentioned this to them. They shrugged. Carolyn leaned forward. "Everyone has computers, don't they?" I held my lips together.

"How is it a non-profit?" I asked, leaning forward. I still was not wrapping my head around this position. I thought I would be working with children or maybe helping with policy.

"It's the research," Carolyn answered, clasping her hands together. "For the position, we're really looking for someone who's local, who knows something about children and can help us make those connections to donors. Do you think that could be you, Denise?" Nope, this was not what I thought it really was. Inwardly I sank. I didn't want to do this kind of work.

Again, I just blinked, unsure how to respond. This was not going well. The disgusting hotdog in my backseat was calling me. Maybe the other interview would be better?

The two women walked me to the elevator. Carolyn promised that she would call me next week, after all the other interviews were complete. I thanked her for her time, extending my hand. I forgot about the awkwardness at the beginning of the interview.

She looked down at me hand. "How quaint! I have a good feeling about you, Denise." She did not shake my hand. I watched the two women wave as the elevator doors closed, grateful to leave.

Chapter 15

I arrived at Café Du Monde at 9:55. Again I went through the trauma of putting on the hot dog costume. Someone would need to burn this costume after I was finished with it.

A member of the film crew arranged the extras at tables at Café Du Monde. They positioned me next to a street musician. Again, I supposed that I would be flailing around, but I waited for the shoot to begin. For right now, I was allowed to drink some coffee. I held it between my gigantic white palms.

Members of the crew set up the camera on the sidewalk in front of the café. Other assistants milled around, checking their phones, staring at the door of the large trailer parked on Decatur Street. They were waiting for something.

One of the members of the crew chattered into her headset and walked past. I caught her eye. "Hey, what's going on?" She held up one finger while she listened to whoever was speaking in her ear.

"The producer is on set today and may stay through the end of shooting. It's good!" She gave me a thumbs up. I lifted my coffee in salute and took another sip.

At last, there was a collective gasp as the trailer door opened and the elf director emerged. A huge grin was plastered on his face. Instead of his usual casual attire, he was wearing a blue blazer over a polo shirt and khaki slacks. A petite woman followed him down the steps. She looked amazing; her peroxide-blond tresses framed her perfectly smooth face. Huge black sunglasses hid her eyes.

She looked like she'd just walked off the page of a Talbot's catalogue. Was she going to a garden party after this? Well, if she was, she looked amazing!

The crew immediately moved closer and she greeted them like a queen greeting her subjects after her long absence. I could hear people murmuring: "So good to see you, Mrs. Murphy," or "Did you have a good flight, Mrs. Murphy?" or "How long will you be with us?" I finally realized that this must be the elf's wife. Wow, he really married up or she really married down, I thought uncharitably.

She moved gracefully around the set, stopping at each table and greeting the extras. She stopped and asked people questions. She was so charming and engaging. Yep, she definitely got the short end of the stick when it came to husbands.

Finally, she made her way to where I was. I could get an even better look at her. I wondered how old she was. She had no wrinkles, but somehow she felt wise and motherly and everything I would like to be when I grow up.

"Hello there, my name is Nadine Murphy. What's your name?" She smiled at me warmly and genuinely. I smiled back at her.

"My name's Denise. Are you in the movie too, Mrs. Murphy?" At my question, she let out a squeal of laughter and shook her head.

"Aren't you sweet? No, I just produce them now for my sweetie." She absently touched the pendant handing around her neck and looked toward the elf in the same way that I look at petit fours.

At that moment, I recognized her. Nadine Murphy was Nadine Quinn! I remembered her from her five or six movies in the early 90's. Nadine Quinn was heir to the Quinn Electric Industry fortune and was often seen in the same circles as the Vanderbilt and Getty families. She was a Paris Hilton before Paris Hilton.

I remembered some of the famous incidents with her. She was supposedly wild at parties, jealous about her boyfriends and always throwing money around. Her escapades with boyfriends sang like the Taylor Swift song catalogue. Unlike Paris Hilton, she was actually amazing as an actress. She could dive into almost any role from comedy to drama while her hair remained perfect. She was poised to be the next Meg Ryan, but she disappeared from Hollywood. I guess now I knew where she went.

"Oh my gosh, I remember you! You were in *Getaway Girl* and also that film about Shakespeare." Nadine Murphy raised both of her hands and then clasped them together. Her smile was radiantly white. "I wish you were still in movies!"

"Oh, thank you. Thank you. Maybe I will sneak back into one, just for you." She reached out and patted my huge gloved hand and chuckled. The transformation from party girl to Princess Grace was complete!

"What a beautiful necklace! I swear I must have missed the memo. I feel like I see that style every time I turn around. What is it?" Mrs. Murphy dropped her hand from her neck and I could see the familiar pendant clearly. I had seen it before, a gold seashell. This one was a scallop shell.

"Michael got me this for our anniversary as a reminder of the month we spent off the Amalfi Coast last year. I designed it and he had it made just for me." I looked at the shell and pressed my lips together. From the corner of my eye, I could see Claudia only a few feet behind Mrs. Murphy. Her eyes looked like they were about to bulge out and explode from behind her tiny glasses. She shifted her scarf to cover her neck.

"Wow, I feel like I see your design everywhere. Have you always designed jewelry? Are you doing that now instead of acting?" I asked. She looked at me blankly.

"Oh no, this is the only one. There's only one in the world. Michael is so romantic. He was even able to get Welch gold, you know, like the Royal Family uses in their wedding rings," she answered. She flitted away toward another crew member. Now I was confused. I had definitely seen the design before. I don't know why, but I had to press the subject.

"There really is only one of those seashell pendants? I thought I saw someone wearing one earlier," I piped up. I opened my mouth and closed it. Mrs. Murphy turned back towards me, her look was puzzled. The director stepped next to his wife and frowned when he saw me.

"Michael, I was just telling Denise about my necklace that I designed and you had made from our vacation in Italy last year. There is only one, right?" She beamed at him. He shook his head silently. He looked at me, his eyes pleaded, and then I realized my blunder.

"I think that's amazing that you designed this piece and there's only one in the world. How romantic!" I chimed in with as much sincerity as I could muster. Look, I know I shouldn't have said it, but again, in my defense, I was dressed as a hotdog. His eyes were tossing daggers at me. He shook his head again and cleared his throat. I nodded and tried to clasp my hands in front of me, but they wouldn't reach. So, I tried leaning on the table beside me and resting my hand. I missed the table and tumbled to the ground.

The director quickly took his wife's elbow and led her away, while she pointed at me, rolling on the ground. He looked over his shoulder at me and I think he mouthed, "thanks," but it might have been something rude. Again, my handlers arrived and lifted me.

Chapter 16

The weekend could not have come sooner. I was thrilled to retire my hotdog costume and wash my hands of show business. On the other hand, perhaps I could have used the experience as a resume builder? Probably not.

On Saturday morning, Emily and I hit Daneel Playground hard. While she hopped, skipped and acted like a monkey, I sat on the park bench and scoured the internet on my phone for information about St. Basil's Church and what they were doing. I wanted to be ready for my interview on Monday.

It seemed like every time I looked down at my phone, Emily would appear right in front of me. I would look up and encourage her back to the slide or swings. She would run to the play structure. I would wave and then look at the phone and once again she would be standing there.

I put down the phone and smiled at Emily. "Okay, honey, what is it?" She reached out her hand and picked up my phone. She looked at it for a moment.

"What are you doing?" she asked sweetly.

"I'm sitting here, watching you on the playground. What do you think I'm doing?" I answered automatically. I didn't understand her question. She could see me right in front of her.

"No, you aren't. You aren't here," she answered. I reached for my phone and she held it behind her back.

"I see. Because I'm on my phone, I'm not paying attention," I said. She took my hand in hers and squeezed it in response.

"You're missing me," she explained, placing her hands on her hips. I was struck with how profound her statement was. I was missing out on what wonderful things Emily was doing because I was not paying attention. I thought I was trying to use my time wisely, instead of wasting time on a park bench, but in fact, I was wasting time I should have been observing and playing with Emily. I took my phone from her and put it in my back pocket. With that, she took my hand and led me around the playground.

During the afternoon, Emily was scheduled to have a play date with her cousin at my sister's house. So I called my friend Carrie and invited her to lunch at Bud's Broiler on City Park Avenue. I hadn't had a chance to speak with Carrie all week. She was in depositions. I was experiencing real life melodrama on the set of the movie.

When I arrived at Bud's, the fragrant odor of barbecue sauce, onions and cooked meat washed over me. I saw Carrie perched on one of the carved up wooden benches next to the juke box. I placed my order and waited to hear my number as I made my way to her.

"So, did you order a hotdog?" Carrie asked with a sly grin. I squinted and pointed at her. We both burst into laughter.

For the next half hour, we ate and laughed as I regaled her with my antics on the set of the movie. I told her about the elfin Michael Murphy and my encounter with Chase Clarke. She sighed with regret at missing her chance to break into Hollywood. After all, she was the one writing a screenplay, not me. I was halfway through a bite of French fries when she asked: "So, what happened with that girl who got attacked?"

I put the other half of the fry down. On a dime, our conversation changed from frivolous to serious. "Who told you about that?"

"Your mom did. She was worried," Carrie answered matter of factly. I chewed the French fry in my mouth and nodded.

"I was worried too. It was scary and I was helpless there on the ground." I looked at my friend. Her perfectly freckled forehead wrinkled with concern. She took my hand and squeezed it. I shrugged my shoulders. "I'm okay, but what does it matter?"

Carrie looked like I might have slapped her across the face, "What do you mean 'what does it matter'? Of course it matters! Some psycho stabbed a woman in front of you! Is she okay? What did the police say? Have they arrested someone?" Carrie was red in the face and almost breathing fire.

"Carrie, I didn't mean to be flip. I guess I don't know what to think." I tried to take a bite of my burger but my appetite suddenly seemed to disappear. "I don't know. It seems like they think she was attacked by 'her pimp' or someone connected to her job. I'm not sure the police are taking it very seriously. What can I do?" I asked Carrie, but I knew that I could do something. I could do more. I just wasn't sure yet what I would do.

"You can be her friend," Carried answered quietly. She took a huge bite of her burger and stared me down from behind the bun. I guess I could do something.

I changed the subject, "I have two interviews. Actually, I just had an interview and I have another one on Monday." Carrie perked up and peppered me with questions.

I described the interview to Carrie and she howled with laughter. I probably should have been offended, but the interview had been pretty funny. I described what Carolyn had said and how I'd answered, giving Carrie a play by play of what was going on in my head the whole time.

"You know what, Denise? I'm going to add that to the screenplay!" Carrie knocked on the table triumphantly.

"Make sure that you emphasize the 'grandmotherly' qualities of your heroine." I retorted. We both giggled.

"What about the other interview?" Carrie asked, after she stopped laughing. I shrugged my shoulders.

"It sounds like they want someone to help them with outreach and that's something I would like to do, but I don't know much about the place except from the internet and Rev. Foucher's 'kind' assessment." I didn't know too much about St. Basil's Church or Rev. Kent.

"I know that it'll be a good interview," Carrie predicted.

"Really, how do you know?" I wondered how Carrie could be so sure.

"Because it has to be better than the last interview!" Again we laughed and finished our burgers. For another thirty minutes, we spoke about some touches to her screenplay. I told her about Jason giving my number to Brock and being weird. She told me about her latest boyfriend. My meal with Carrie was just what I needed.

I returned to the house after lunch and perched on the front porch swing. I still had an hour before I had to pick up my daughter. The street was busy, neighbors were working on their yards and I just swung back and forth. I heard my phone ding. A text came into my phone. I did not recognize the number. It read simply: "Hello Denise."

I texted back: "Who is this?"

"Brock, from the Riverwalk with Jason, I sat next to you!" I read the text. There were about six exclamation points and I think an emoji with its tongue hanging out.

"Hello, Brock, how are you?" I texted back and waited. I stared down at the screen, but nothing popped up. So, this was what entering the dating pool was like? Texting and waiting for texts? Ugh!

The phone dinged again: "Fine." I let my head fall back on the swing and groaned. I looked down again. Nothing, nothing, nothing…

"Do you want to get some coffee sometime?" the phone asked with a dozen question marks.

I thought about my response. I actually thought about it. Did I want to get coffee with Brock? He was kind of cute. He seemed pretty nice.

"Okay," I typed back.

"Cool" and that was it. I waited another ten minutes and still there was no response. Maybe I was not cut out for modern dating. A horn honked on the street and my mind returned to the present. Somehow, my time seemed better spent sitting on that porch swing than texting.

Finally the phone rang, I picked up. "Uh, hey, this is, uh, Brock." I could hear the uncertainty in Brock's voice. He was actually nervous.

"Hello, Brock. It's nice to talk to you." I spoke reassuringly. I leaned back in the swing and it started to move.

"I thought it would be better to actually speak with you, but I have to be honest. I'm not really great at this. Do you want to meet for a drink tonight? I drink a lot of coffee, maybe a drink is better? If you're busy, I understand. I don't want to bother you." I could almost see him pacing back and forth. I think that maybe he'd had a little too much java today.

"That sounds lovely. Where should we meet and what time?" I could hear him holding a hand over his phone. He spoke sharply with someone else.

"Uh, I don't know. I don't really drink. Maybe could I take you to dinner? Excuse me one moment." Again, the phone was muffled, but I could tell he was definitely arguing with someone, trying to quiet the other person down.

"That sounds fine. I would like that. Again, where should we meet and what time?" I asked and waited.

"Let's meet at Taqueria Corona's on Magazine Street. Don't you live Uptown?" he asked. I wondered how much he already knew about me.

"Yes, I do live Uptown. I will see you at Taqueria, but at what time?" I asked.

"See you at 6:45 p.m.! Bye, Denise!" He hung up before I could finish uttering "goodbye." His nervousness was charming, but a little bit annoying.

Chapter 17

At 6:45 p.m., I pushed through the double doors of Taqueria Corona. I scanned the room with its pictures of Zapata and decorations of the Mexican Flag. I saw Brock seated at a table near the window. He looked a little more casual than he had when I'd first seen him— a plain grey t-shirt and jeans. He leaned forward and sipped his drink through a straw.

I slipped next to the table. "Hello!" I looked down at him. He immediately shot upwards, holding the straw between his teeth. "I hope I didn't scare you," I said. He took the straw from his mouth and brought his other hand to his forehead.

"No, I've been really looking forward to this today. You look beautiful." With that, he greeted me with a warm hug. I could catch a slight scent of corn chip and Old Spice.

While he was so nervous, somehow I suddenly felt at ease. I sat across from him and eyeballed the basket of chips and pico de gallo on the table. Before I'd left the house, I'd promised myself that I would not pig out on the chips, but he immediately offered them to me.

"You really look great in that color," he said. I looked down at my light blue sweater and jeans. I was delighted that I could actually still zip up these jeans after these last few months.

"Thank you, you're sweet." A little bit of color crept into his cheeks. He let out a breath that he must have been holding for a while. The waitress approached the table and took my drink order. Brock lifted the basket of chips and ordered another along with the queso.

"So, I hear you were a hotdog in a movie. That sounds pretty cool! What was it like?" Brock asked. He leaned forward to listen. His eyes were bright and warm brown. He seemed so genuinely interested in what I was doing. Then it hit me. He was actually interested in me.

I couldn't really remember the last time I'd gone on an official date. I think it might have been before my daughter came into my life. It had to have been at least four or five years ago. How was I supposed to do this?

Now I was feeling nervous. I was starting to sweat. I put down a chip. I might as well get this out of the way.

"Uh, I should tell you that I'm not working. I'm divorced. I'm a single mother. I'm also living with my mother right now." I blurted it all out. Then I wanted to drop my head on the table. I was pretty sure that was not how to do it.

"Is this all in the interest of full disclosure? Because I'm pretty sure that I have a hole in my left sock. I have killed every houseplant that I've ever bought. I also really love *Lord of the Rings*." With his declaration, we both laughed. I leaned back and looked at his feet.

"So, just your left sock? Because I cannot deal with holes in the right sock," I said, wagging a finger. Again we laughed. The waitress took our order and the meal progressed splendidly. We both joked and talked easily.

He was about to tell me a story about his younger brother, when something caught his eye behind me. He peered out the window at something or someone. I craned my neck to look, but I couldn't see anything.

"What is it?" I asked. Cars passed on Magazine Street. A couple of people walked down the sidewalk. I didn't see what held his attention.

He sipped his drink and shook his head. "It's probably nothing." He tried to concentrate on his food, but again he looked out the window. Finally, I turned around completely.

"What are you looking at?" I asked. I turned back to him and he pressed his lips together.

"I just thought that I saw someone outside who was familiar, but then I thought that's kind of weird. It couldn't be him." Again he returned to his tacos and resumed telling the story. I listened attentively. Suddenly, his eyes grew large.

I turned around just in time to see Jason Stone strolling down Magazine Street toward the front door of the restaurant. He opened the door and entered. Brock slumped a little in his chair.

He walked right up to the table and looked down at Brock and me. "What are you two doing here?" He smirked at Brock.

Brock glared at Jason and shook his head, "We're having dinner. What does it look like? Do you want to join us?" I knew the last question was actually rhetorical, but Jason stood up a little straighter.

"Sure, I'd love to." To Brock and my wide-eyed surprise, Jason pulled a chair from the adjoining table and sat down with us. He waved to the waitress and ordered a Dos Equis. Brock was dumfounded, but I wasn't.

"What are you doing here?" I asked Jason. I knew that Brock wanted to know the answer as well. For that matter, I think he actually just wanted Jason to leave.

"I was in the neighborhood and I'd just been to the park." I nodded, listening to his story. It didn't take a detective to know that something about his words wasn't adding up. I looked out the window. It was dark.

"Jason, you were in the park this late and just now you're walking home?" I interrogated. He sipped his beer and shook his head. Now, I knew this was a lie because anytime I'd seen Jason in the park, he was running, without a shirt. Now he was in jeans and a sweatshirt. I pushed ahead, "You were jogging in jeans?"

He looked down at his outfit and turned his head to one side. He refused to answer my question. I pressed on, "I didn't know that you lived around here."

"He doesn't," Brock answered icily. Brock's stare bore into Jason. What was going on? Jason reached across the table grabbed a chip, dipping it in the queso. Was this a Mexican food standoff?

"I was just in the neighborhood. I'd been to the park. I saw you two and just wanted to say 'hi'" He spoke calmly. He looked into my eyes. I had to slap a hand across my mouth to keep from laughing.

"Were you checking up on us?" I asked. Jason huffed and sat up straighter. Brock looked across at me and raised an approving eyebrow.

"He should keep an eye on you," Brock said and he winked at me. He sounded like a leering old man. Jason and I both looked at Brock. Jason sat back and finished his beer. Still he was quiet.

"Like I said, I was in the neighborhood," he answered. I wanted to wring his neck at the answer. The waitress approached the table. He looked back at me. He turned to the waitress and ordered!

He leaned back in his chair. "So, what's Emily doing tonight, Denise?" Jason asked. Brock's eyes were like saucers.

"She's with her babysitter, probably watching Daniel Tiger and eating ravioli," I answered. I thought for a moment about Emily, sitting in her footie pajamas, watching her favorite show. It took me a moment to wonder if Jason was trying to tank my date with Brock? Jason shifted his focus to Brock, waiting for a response.

"She sounds sweet," Brock responded enthusiastically. He looked to me for reassurance.

"She's a sweet little girl and very friendly. I like her," Jason said to Brock. This time I stared at Jason. What was going on? He returned the stare. "How's your mother doing? I haven't seen her in a while. Everything going okay at the house?"

I clenched my teeth together. He *was* trying to tank my date! Why? He was the one who'd set us up! "My mother's doing fine. Also, I think that my athlete's foot fungus has cleared up as well." Brock snorted from across the table. Jason let out a little laugh.

We finished our meal in almost silence. Jason talked about his thoughts on a case that his division had just finished with. Brock reverted to only speaking when I asked him questions. Both almost lunged for the check at the end.

I looked down at my watch. I needed to get home, and yet, I was just a little curious about being the fly on the wall when I left. I stood up to leave.

"Denise, let me drive you home," Brock offered. The evening had started fairly well and then had descended into utter weirdness. I shook my head.

"I walked actually. It really isn't that far from the house. I think I'll walk back." I started to head to the door. I looked at Brock. He was disappointed. "Thank you, Brock. I had a good time."

Before either man could stop me, I rushed for the door and headed down Magazine Street. I turned right on Eleanor Street and stopped. At first I started to laugh. The situation was so weird. Then I started to cry. Why had Jason shown up like that? I wiped the tears from my eyes and kept walking down the street towards Constance Street.

I heard something behind me. It sounded like someone stepping on some branches. I moved a little faster. "Hey, Denise." I turned to the sound of the voice.

Jason walked up next to me. I looked up at him. His expression changed from a smirk to concern. "Were you crying?"

I rolled my eyes and turned to walk away. He grabbed my arm and pulled me back. Now the waterworks were starting. I wasn't even sure why. "You're crying. Why are you crying?" I tried to pull away, but he refused to let go of my arm.

"Why did you show up tonight?" I asked him. I wanted to know. His hand dropped from my arm. He stepped closer to me.

"I don't know," he said softly.

"We were on a date. You know that, right? Is that so hard to believe about me? That someone might find me desirable? Why did you bring up those things about Emily and my mom? You didn't do that because you cared about them at all. You were doing that just to be mean!" I stepped back from him. I felt so hurt and angry.

"I just didn't like seeing..." He stopped talking. He put his hands in his back pockets and rocked back. "I'm sorry," he mumbled.

"And if you didn't want me to go on a date with him, why didn't you say something?" He was silent. In the light from the streetlamp, I could see that he was breathing deeply. "Why don't you say something?"

I couldn't see his eyes because they were so downcast. I looked down at the ground and wiped tears away. I sighed and almost on cue I felt his hands holding my cheeks. He positioned my head so that I looked up into his eyes and I felt his lips.

His lips pressed against mine and softly he kissed me. I could feel lightning zing through my veins. My eyes closed and almost as soon as the kiss started, he pulled away. His hands dropped to his side. He turned and looked towards Magazine Street.

"I better go. Good night, Denise." With that, he left me on Eleanor Street in a complete daze. I watched as his long legs carried him quickly to Magazine Street. Had I just imagined it or had Jason Stone just kissed me?

"Wait, what was that?" I called after Jason, but I was just shouting at his shadow. I touched my lips. They felt warm and I could almost smell his scent of leather and woods, but he was gone. I clutched my purse to me and made my way to Constance Street and took a left, heading to the house.

Chapter 18

The rest of the weekend felt like a blur. My mind would drift back to that moment on Eleanor Street and the feel of Jason's hands holding my cheeks. On Sunday evening, I received a text from Brock wondering if I would like to try our date again. I texted my friend Carrie about the situation. All she would reply is that she wanted to use this in her screenplay. I wondered how much wine was permissible for one woman to drink. I actually wondered if maybe I should just start drinking wine.

Monday morning I drove Emily to pre-school. She and I chatted and sang songs along the way. She asked me to pretend that there was a kitty cat in the backseat and I feigned surprise when she started to meow.

"You know that it was me? I was the kitty cat!" Emily explained with great earnestness. I smiled and looked into the mirror as we rode along. Emily was thoughtful for a moment and watched a streetcar roll past us in traffic.

"Where are you going today, Mommy?" Emily asked.

"I have an interview for a job," I answered matter of factly.

"What do you do?" Emily asked, her little brow wrinkled as she listened.

"Well, I hope that it will be a position at a church where I assist people in finding meaningful ministry and outreach." As soon as the answer left my lips, I could see Emily crinkle her nose. I made no sense at all. I released a sigh. "I want to help people."

"Like you do with the hotdog?" Emily asked hopeful. I thought about it a moment.

"That's a temporary job. I'm just dressing up as a hotdog in a movie," I tried to explain. Emily shook her head.

"You are helping people!" she proclaimed. I decided that I wouldn't argue with a four year old. We arrived at St. Mary's School and I dropped her off in her classroom.

She squeezed me tightly and whispered: "You always help people, Mommy! I love you!" With that, she ran into her spot on the mat in the room. I bit the inside of my cheek to keep from tearing up and left.

Chapter 19

After dropping off Emily, I had about two hours until my interview with Rev. Kent at St. Basil's Church. I drove to John Jay on St. Charles Avenue and got a haircut. I emerged with gorgeous layers, held in place with probably a whole can of hair spray. If I didn't get this position, at least my hair looked really good.

Afterwards, I drove back to the house, but as I drove I could smell what I can only describe as mud and soggy foam hotdog coming from the backseat of my car. The stink was getting worse somehow. I'd wondered why Emily kept asking me to open the windows. Now I understood.

I rolled into the Safari Car Wash on Claiborne, choosing the cheapest wash. After going through the carwash, I pulled into the vacuuming area and hopped out and began to vacuum. First I went to my side. I opened the back and discovered a thousand goldfish and maybe an M and M mashed into Emily's seat. I vacuumed as much as I could.

I moved to the front passenger side of my Honda. I opened the door. Before I could vacuum, I had to pick up a few papers from the floor. As soon as I picked up the sheets, something on the floorboard shined in the sunlight. I reached down and picked up a gold necklace with a sea shell pendant. I turned it over in my hand. Where had this come from?

It looked familiar. On closer inspection, I knew it was not one of Emily's toy necklaces. It was a delicate gold chain and an intricately designed piece of jewelry.

I shook my head remembering my conversation with Mrs. Murphy on the movie set. This was the same design. This was the same *pendant*. How had this gotten in my car?

I remembered Lacy dumping over her purse when she'd sat here. It must have been *her* necklace. I reached into my car for my phone, but I realized that I didn't have her phone number. When she'd called me, she'd called *her* cellphone and called from the hospital. I groaned loudly. Was I destined to keep holding onto Lacy's possessions forever?

I looked up the phone number for Bad Daddy's and hoped someone nice would answer the phone and that Lacy would be there. The phone rang twice, and at last someone answered, "Bad Daddy's, how can I help you?" The voice was actually somewhat chipper.

"Yes, may I speak with Lacy?" I asked. I waited for some rude response.

"Whom may I say is calling?" Wow! For a sleazy strip joint whoever their receptionist was, she was great on a telephone.

"It's Denise Reed, her friend from the movie." I was immediately put on hold. The hold music was "Joyful, joyful." At this point, I was filled with so many questions, but they'd have to wait when I heard Lacy's voice on the line.

"Hey, Denise, what's up?" she asked. I could tell by her tone that she was pretty busy.

"Hi, Lacy, I found your necklace in my car. Do you want me to bring it to you?" I wondered just how many times I'd be driving into the Quarter this week. I heard her suck in a breath.

"I wondered where that went. Yeah, I guess so. Would you be able to bring it down here this afternoon?" she asked hopefully. I thought about going back to Bad Daddy's and a shiver ran down my spine.

Would I run into her scary boss? Would my feet stick to the floor? I also didn't have anything left in my purse to clean out if I needed to escape quickly.

"Sure. I'll drop it off after 3 p.m." I looked down at my watch. Yikes, I was cutting it close. I needed to head home, clean up and change before my interview.

"Thanks. See you then!" she answered and then hung up. I finished cleaning my car and headed home.

Chapter 20

At 10 minutes to my appointment, I pulled into the parking lot across the street from St. Basil's Episcopal Church in Metairie. The church was a huge 1950's A-frame church with a huge stained-glass window that faced Metairie Road. I tried to determine what the image was, but I couldn't tell from the outside and, frankly, I needed to hurry up and get inside.

With five minutes to spare, I was already seated at a long wooden table in a conference room in St. Basil's Church with a glass of water, waiting for my interview. Despite the comfortable spot, I tried not to squirm in my chair. I pulled at the bottom of my grey jacket and wiped away an invisible speck of lint. I inspected the hem of my skirt. Was that a string? Don't pull on it, don't pull on it!

I looked around the room, checking out the pictures. One wall was filled with different photos of various folks in the congregation at different events. One was either a crawfish boil or a barbecue, another was children in a Christmas pageant, and the others were candid photographs of people drinking coffee or sitting in church. On the other wall was a framed poster with a quotation from Julian of Norwich: "All shall be well, and all shall be well, and all manner of thing shall be well." I smiled to myself, thinking of how many times my mother had quoted that beloved line.

"Hello, Denise, I'm so glad to meet you at last!" I immediately turned toward the voice and stood, bumping the table and knocking over my glass of water, as I reached out to shake Rev. Kent's hand. For a moment, we both looked down at the spill and a smile of delight crept across his face. He took my hand and pumped it twice.

"It's so nice to meet you. Do you have a paper towel?" I asked and inwardly groaned. My first impression with a possible employer after months of not working and not getting interviews is that I'm a complete and utter klutz. I tried to maintain my composure, but I wanted to just curl onto the floor and sob.

I looked at Rev. Kent. His expression was so kind. He was in his mid 60's, grey hair and balding, wearing a navy suit and his clerical collar. He reminded me of a doctor in a Norman Rockwell painting. He turned from looking at the table and called to someone else in the office: "Hey, Valerie, I need some paper towels in here!"

"You know, one time when I was interviewing for a position, I managed to squirt all of the ink out of my fountain pen onto the interviewer. Needless to say, the gentleman was very perturbed and I was not invited to work as a lifeguard at Pinewood Country Club that summer." He smiled and started to laugh. Suddenly, my mood lifted. Maybe it would be okay. I started to laugh too.

"Have you been to St. Basil's before? Let me take you around and then we can go grab an early lunch!" With that, I followed him through the church. We moved briskly down a hallway as he pointed out two classrooms, a bathroom, offices, a kitchen, large meeting room, and another hallway which housed a preschool. Finally we turned another corner and entered the sanctuary of the church.

The sanctuary was modern, with varying shades of beige and cypress pews. On the wall facing Metairie

Road was a colorful stained-glass window. It was pretty abstract. I squinted to try to make out what the image was.

"It's based on the fresco of Basil the Great in the cathedral of Ohrid in Macedonia. He's celebrating the Holy Eucharist and leaning over the table." He mimicked the posture for me, leaning forward and pressing his hands together in a prayer pose. Rev. Kent straightened up and rubbed his hands together in excitement as he led me towards the wall beneath the window. There was a framed print of what he was talking about. To be honest, I still couldn't see what he was talking about, but I don't know much about abstract art.

"Tell me, Denise, do you know who St. Basil is?" Rev. Kent asked seriously.

"A Cappadocian father, a doctor of the church." I patted myself on my back for actually re-reading one of my college text books.

"Yes, he was a great theologian, but he was also passionate and served the poor," Rev. Kent replied. He pressed his lips together like he was either stifling a frown or laugh. "Let's go to lunch!"

Chapter 21

At lunch, he chattered about the history of the church and the story of St. Basil in more detail. Every now and then asking a question and thoughtfully responding to my answers. Rev. Kent had chosen a delicious Italian restaurant/Po-boy place on Bonnabel. I had ordered a roast beef, dressed, but I could hardly touch it. Delicious brown gravy dripped from the sides of the crunchy French bread. The lunch looked delicious, but I tried to control myself from eating too much and possibly dropping something on my lap or knocking anything else over. I tried eating with a fork, but somehow that seemed a little silly as well.

While I was nervous, I couldn't help but enjoy myself. I listened to Rev. Kent's many funny anecdotes about his time at St. Basil's. He told me stories about his growing up and his call to the ministry. He was fascinating!

"So, what went down at your other church?" The question caught me off guard. I blinked and stuttered. Great, now I was going to blow it.

"I spoke with Rev. Foucher about all you did there and I'm wondering why you left." He looked at me thoughtfully. He was quiet for a moment, "I've been at this for a long time. I'm retiring in about two years. There's not much you could say that would shock me."

I could feel a tear welling in the corner of my eye. I wondered how to phrase this. Would I give him a perfectly political answer? How could I make this sound better?

I blurted out the truth: "I talked myself out of the position. I knew that I wanted to do something really meaningful, but I wasn't sure what. I started talking to Rev. Foucher and next thing I knew I was out of a job." I looked down at my hands.

"It sounds like you feel pretty embarrassed about that. I know that feeling, but let me ask you something else. Am I correct that you weren't happy there?" he asked. I nodded. "Maybe it doesn't feel like it right now, but you know, if we're lucky, we actually learn more from our mistakes than we learn from our successes."

"I guess, but I'm not sure what I'm learning right now," I answered with a mirthless laugh. He was quiet for a moment, pressing his lips together as if considering what he wanted to say.

"What have you been doing since leaving St. Christopher's?" he asked cheerfully. I thought about being vague, but something about him drew out honesty.

"Lately, I've been working some odd jobs. I worked at Riverview retirement home. This last week I've been working as an extra in a movie. I was actually a hotdog—a Lucky Dog, in particular." Rev. Kent's eyes grew wide with delight.

"Why, Denise, that sounds terrible, but really funny!" He slapped a hand over his mouth to muffle his laughter. He looked at me. "I'm sorry. I shouldn't laugh. You know, I spent one summer working in a country western restaurant where I had to dress like Howdy Doody, so I know a little bit of the pain." Now, I was laughing too. "I was no more a cowboy than I suspect you were a hotdog, but you have to do what you have to do!"

At that moment, I couldn't believe how happy I was to meet Rev. Kent. I wanted the position, if only to listen to his stories. Frankly, I realized that no matter how it went today, I was glad that I was there. He dabbed his mouth and his expression grew more serious.

"I suspect you're learning a great deal right now. I have a feeling that someone as remarkable as you is learning a lot and those lessons and skills are going to help you do something amazing." He smiled a kind, grandfatherly smile. "So, what would you like to do?" He leaned closer.

"I would like to serve. I want to help people." This was not what I had rehearsed in my mirror last night, but it was true. I thought back to my exchange that morning with Emily, my heart warmed with the thought of her words of encouragement. Rev. Kent leaned back in his chair and crossed his arms.

Rev. Kent thought about my words. "That's exactly how I see this position, Denise. I want someone to help us discover what the needs are of this community. I know that people think that there aren't any people in need in Old Metairie, but there are. The hard part around here is finding the resources and making people aware of those resources."

"Do you mean that the different organizations don't know about each other?" I asked. I leaned closer. This position was getting really interesting.

"That is exactly what I mean! One organization doesn't know what the other organization does, so we can end up duplicating effort or missing a need completely. The other side I see is that I want us to do something meaningful in our community. I want us to help in a way that lifts up our community." Rev. Kent was getting really excited about this. Frankly, so was I. It sounded cool!

"I could do that. A lot would be making connections with people, calling folks," I thought aloud. Rev. Kent nodded.

He pointed at me and then brought his finger to his lips, "Denise, I have a good feeling about you." I almost laughed when he said the words. I contrasted them with Carolyn at Education Tree. Both had a good feeling about me, but really the question was who did *I* have a good feeling about?

After we finished our lunch, we returned to St. Basil's Church. Rev. Kent shook my hand and thanked me for the interview, promising to call the following week with his decision for the position. For the first time, in a long time, I felt really good about an interview.

Chapter 22

I sat in my car in the small parking lot at St. Basil's. I don't want to reveal just how many times I replayed "Eye of the Tiger" on my iPhone, but it was more than twice. I looked down at my watch. It was 2:30 and it would probably take 30 minutes to enter the French Quarter again and find a place to park. I groaned. I pulled Lacy's necklace from my purse, examining it in the light.

The design was beautiful, a delicately carved little shell. I turned it around in my hand. All sides were carved. The chain itself was made of the thinnest gold, maybe 20 inches. I almost overlooked it, but within the carving of the shell itself, I read four letters, a plus sign between them. It read: "M.M. plus N.M." Indeed, this was Nadine Murphy's necklace, but something told me that the elf director had not had just one made. What a jerk!

I thought about going to Bad Daddy's alone, but I decided that I needed some backup. I also thought about standing on the sidewalk of Eleanor Street with Jason. It felt like a kiss, but I still didn't know what it meant. It might be nice to hang out a little bit with Jason. I was sure that he would love to accompany me to a strip club. I dialed his cell.

"This is Stone." I wondered if he did or did not have my number saved in his cellphone. My guess was either no or he was in the middle of a meeting.

"Uh, yes, it's Denise." I was now unsure if I should bother him. I wondered if he'd ask, "Denise who?"

"Yes, Denise, what can I assist you with?" Okay, there must have been other people around or he was being the biggest jerk possible. He was definitely busy, but still willing to take my call.

"I was wondering if you would come with me to Big Daddy's?" I heard a huff at the other end of the phone.

"Denise, would you give me a moment please?" I overheard him excusing himself from some people. I waited. It sounded like he was moving boxes. Suddenly he came back on the line, "Why in the world would you go back to that place?"

"I need to return a necklace to Lacy. She dropped it in my car," I answered apologetically.

"Denise, that place is filled with shady and dangerous people. Probably the person who stabbed Lacy is there. You can't go in there!" He was almost shouting into the phone. I held my cell away from my ear. Yikes!

"I know that, Jason. That's why I am calling you. You're my back-up. I just need to drop off this necklace, but I want to be able to ask Lacy a couple of questions too." I knew as soon as I'd said what I said that he was super angry.

"I'm your 'back-up!' Wait, what questions are you going to ask her? And if she won't talk to Detective Antoine, why would she talk to you?" He made some valid points. Perhaps I shouldn't have called him my "back-up." Maybe he was more like my arm candy? I should have called him my arm candy.

"I have a few questions about this necklace and who gave it to her. She'll talk to me because I'm a friend," I answered. I could hear him huffing on the other end.

"All right; we'll park at the New Orleans Athletic Club lot on Rampart. I'll see you there in 30 minutes."

He hung up.

Chapter 22

I made it to the parking lot at the NOAC in 20 minutes and found a spot on the very top floor. I looked around the lot, realizing that I had no idea what Jason's car looked like. For that matter, we'd never confirmed where we'd meet in the lot. Should I stay put? Should I start walking down to the first level?

I heard a rumble coming up the ramp. A sleek black motorcycle pulled into the spot next to my car. Its rider removed black and red helmet. Of course, he rode a motorcycle—or as my friends in college used to call them—a crotch rocket.

I got out of my car and smiled broadly at Jason. He just shook his head. He was pissed. It was as if he'd completely forgotten about what had happened when he'd kissed me. For that matter, maybe I had imagined it.

"For the record, I still think this is a stupid idea. There's no reason to go to that place," he said as he stuffed his helmet into the compartment on the back of his bike.

"That's the response from someone who just got off a death machine," I retorted. I leaned against my car and waited for him to finish putting away his gear.

"So, you won't take a ride with me?" My mouth practically fell open. Was he offering? He laughed. I laughed trying to cover my complete lust.

He finally turned in my direction and looked directly at me. He cocked his head slightly to the left. His gaze traveled from the top of my head to my toes. He sucked in a breath. He wanted to say something, but stopped himself. "Wow!" was all he mustered.

"Wow, what?" I asked, ready for some compliment. For what might have been the first time in my life my hair was behaving, my suit appeared crisp and, frankly, I had it going on! I waited.

"Uh." I waited. "Nothing. Let's go!" The moment was lost. With a turn of the heel, we took off towards Bad Daddy's. I have long legs, but Jason was almost flying through the Quarter. He wove through buggies, tourists, and uneven sidewalks like a speed walking champion. I huffed and puffed behind him, trying to keep up.

At last, we arrived at the front door of Bad Daddy's. Once again, the muscle mountain in neon was perched on a stool next to the door, head down, reading something. I could sense Jason beside me tensing up. I placed a hand on his arm, stopping him.

"Hello there! I'm here to see Lacy." I smiled brightly at the bouncer. He quickly closed his book and again stuffed the paperback in the waistband of his tight jean shorts. I caught the title, Robert Fulghum's, *All I Really Need to Know I Learned in Kindergarten*. Wow! Who was this bouncer? I would never have expected someone who looked as much like a rock to read such thoughtful books, but you know the old saying about judging book covers, or mountains. I couldn't help but comment, "How do you like this book? Aren't his essays cute?"

Again, the bouncer turned a little pink and ignored my question. He leaned from his stool towards the door and pulled it open. He gave some sort of man nod to Jason and Jason returned it, as we entered the club.

Not much had changed since I'd last visited. In fact, it appeared the same. Five or six guys were scattered around black lacquer tables totally engrossed in their phones, and the dancers were on break again. The music was turned down, but still emanated a thumping beat. We walked toward the back hallway and I went to the dressing room, knocking on the door.

The door swung open again. This time a woman with wavy, shoulder length brown highlighted hair and not much else on opened the door. She looked totally past me and winked at Jason. "What can I do for you, honey?" she asked with a slight country twang.

I cleared my throat and answered her: "I'm looking for Lacy. Is she here?" The woman looked Jason up and down. To his credit, his eyes appeared not to look down and he focused on her face.

Finally, she turned to look at me, "She isn't performing tonight."

"But isn't she here? I was supposed to meet her," I said. She flicked her hair, almost exposing herself.

"Yeah, she's waitressing. She's in Mr. Gicardo's office." She pointed to the office down the hallway. "I can entertain your friend while you go see her, if you want." She gave Jason a wicked grin.

"That's so kind," I answered with faux sincerity. She shrugged at me and then closed the door. Jason lingered a little too long at the closed door. "Jason!" He seemed to snap out of the chestnut vixen's spell and turned around. I waved him toward me and we walked to the other door, across the hallway.

I tapped softly on the door. I could hear some talking behind it. Again, I tapped. Jason looked down at me and rolled his eyes. He reached over and pounded on the door. Immediately, the door swung open, "What?" barked from behind the door.

Mr. Gicardo opened the door wide and stared at me and then turned his attention to Jason. "I didn't do nothing!" He attempted to close the door, but Jason stepped forward. I sensed someone standing behind us. It was the mountain, balling his hands into meaty fists.

"Wait, Al, that's my friend Denise." I heard Lacy's voice from behind Mr. Gicardo. Again, he looked at me. Brown eyes and bushy greying eyebrows opened wide. He remembered who I was.

"You handed me a sanitary pad!" H said it as if I'd stolen his car or kicked his kitten. Jason leaned in toward the man, as if he was ready to put him in a headlock, when he looked down at me.

"You handed him a maxi-pad? Why would you do that?" he asked incredulously. His face scrunched in disgust.

"It wasn't used!" I defended myself to Jason and then turned to Mr. Gicardo, "Yes, I did it because you were being scary!" Yeah, take that! I couldn't think of anything better to say at that moment. I heard Lacy's laughter. She ducked under one of Mr. Gicardo's arms.

She was wearing a tight see-through white t-shirt with a pink bra underneath and Daisy Dukes that would have made Daisy Duke banned from television. Her hair was in two braids to her shoulders. Her cheeks and eyelids were hidden under gobs of glitter.

Again, Jason and Mr. Gicardo exchanged some sort of man nod, this time with a grunt. They both stepped back. The mountain crossed his enormous arms across his chest and leaned back against the wall. Lacy stood between the two men and smiled at both of them.

"I have your necklace that you dropped in my car." I reached into my purse and looked over to Mr. Gicardo. He suddenly stepped back and started shrinking into his office, afraid of what I might pull out this time. I carefully placed the necklace in Lacy's hand.

Lacy's smile dropped as I handed her the necklace. She looked sad. Mr. Gicardo instinctively reached out and patted Lacy softly on the shoulder.

"You should tell that no good jerk that you'll send this to his wife if he don't give you some cash. That's what you should do with that thing!" Mr. Gicardo exclaimed. You could see the gears moving in his head about this idea.

"Except that's illegal, and I'm sure that Lacy or you would never do anything illegal at Bad Daddy's," Jason spoke. Mr. Gicardo looked at Jason and shifted his weight on his feet. Mr. Gicardo lifted his hands, palms up, as if proclaiming his innocence.

"Of course not. We run a clean business here. I'm just saying that it's all his fault that Lacy's hurt, that's all. If I see that shrimp again, I'll kick his tiny a—" Lacy took hold of Mr. Gicardo's arm and shook her head.

"Thanks for bringing it to me, Denise." She smiled at me and then slipped the necklace into the pocket of her shorts. I smiled at Lacy.

"Lacy, if your boyfriend was the one who attacked you, you need to tell the police. Did he?" I asked her. Her face went blank. Her eyes flicked over to Jason. Jason lifted his chin and leaned against the wall, waiting to hear her response.

"Let it go, Denise. He didn't do— It's over. Okay?" she said. I caught what she said. So, it wasn't her boyfriend, but he was involved. He didn't do what?

"But..." Lacy turned away from me and headed toward the dressing room. Mr. Gicardo turned his palms up and shrugged his massive shoulders.

I looked at Mr. Gicardo. I remembered that one of the dancers had mentioned something about Lacy's boyfriend being important. He must know.

"Do you know who her boyfriend is? What's his name?" I asked him. He immediately crossed his arms. His stance became belligerent.

"I don't talk to cops." He scowled at Jason. Jason rolled his eyes and stepped away. His phone chirped and he walked a little further down the hall to speak to someone.

"I'm not a cop. Do you *know* who her boyfriend is?" I asked again. He huffed. I reached into my purse. His eyes got bigger.

"Don't you go handing me anything!" he warned, lifting his hands in front of himself in a protective stance.

"Tell me, please," I asked sweetly, but I also kept rummaging in the bag. When had I put a lollipop in my purse? Thankfully it still was in its wrapper.

"I don't know his name actually," he answered sheepishly. I thought about what he'd said earlier.

"But you've seen him?" I asked. He nodded. "Well? What does he look like?" I was pretty sure I knew what the description would be, but I wanted him to confirm it for me.

"I don't know. He's a shrimp. Some twerp. Super snob. That's all I'm telling you. If she don't want me to say nothing about it, I ain't saying nothing." His face bunched up in disgust. I knew a shrimp—rather, I knew an elf. "I think you and your boyfriend should go."

"Before I go, I do have another question for you." I glanced over to the neon mountain leaning against the wall and then back at Mr. Gicardo. "Maybe for you." I addressed the bouncer. He leaned forward a little bit.

"Are you in a book club?" Both Mr. Gicardo and the mountain blushed. "I noticed your books and I just wondered. I kind of like devotional books." At this point, Jason had returned to the conversation. He was completely flummoxed. Again he stepped away. The two other men looked as if they were little boys caught with their hands in a cookie jar.

"Uh, I don't have to answer anymore of these questions. I ain't no wus," Mr. Gicardo proclaimed indignantly. I pulled my hand from my purse, producing a hairy package of gum. I lifted the package toward him, offering him a piece. He immediately stepped back in his office and slammed the door.

I turned toward the bouncer. He raised an eyebrow and silently took a slice of gum that I offered. He opened the gum and plopped it in his mouth, chewing for a moment, and then with a squeaky voice better suited for a cartoon creature replied, "We have book club on Thursday nights at CC's on Royal Street at 7:30 p.m. Our next selection will be *Messy Spirituality* by the late Mike Yacconelli. You have to bring a snack to share." I thanked him. He bowed his head and stomped toward the front door.

I walked next to Jason and signaled him that I wanted to leave. I'd gotten what I came there for, but I wanted to stop one more place in the Quarter just to check my theory. I looked at my watch. 3:30 p.m. I'd need to move quickly before my next stop closed for the day at 4 p.m.

Chapter 23

A few minutes later, Jason and I stood in front of
Duncan Valmont's shop on Bienville Street. I checked
my watch. It was not 4 p.m. yet, but the door was
already locked. I rang the bell and knocked. I could
hear someone inside rummaging around.

At last, I saw Duncan through the window in the
door and waved. He waved back and twisted the lock.
He pulled the door open, put a hand on his hip and
smiled at me.

"Hello there, my Lucky Dog friend!" he exclaimed.
He stepped back and invited Jason and me into the
store. This day the shop smelled of lavender. "What are
you doing here?"

"Hi, Duncan! This is my friend Jason. I was
wondering if you'd help me with something." I looked
at him sweetly.

"It's not illegal, is it?" We both laughed. I noticed
that Jason didn't laugh. He was probably wondering
what he was doing in this store filled with eclectic junk.

"I don't think so, but it is kind of serious. May I see
your security tapes from the night of the stabbing?"
Jason shot a look at me.

"I don't think you should be looking at that. Besides,
I'm sure that Detective Antoine has it," Jason answered
my question. He crossed his arms in disgust.

"No, she didn't want them. They didn't show
anything really." Duncan ignored Jason. He leaned a
little closer to me and whispered in a voice I'm sure

that Jason could hear, "What's with old grumpy muscles?"

"He isn't usually grumpy. It's because he's my back-up," I answered, smiling at Jason who rolled his eyes.

"Ooh, is he a singer?" Duncan asked. At that, Jason released a howl of laughter. In my mind I was imagining Jason singing doo wop behind a 1950's microphone. Apparently, Jason was imagining the same thing. Duncan waved us towards the back of his shop. We followed him.

"You look lovely, by the way. Are you two heading out on a date after this?" He smiled, looking at Jason and me. Jason shook his head vigorously. At least, Duncan thought I looked good.

The back room was tiny and cramped. Stacks of papers covered every open spot, on the top of the desk next to the computer, on top of the computer, on book shelves. Duncan clicked the computer and the screen turned on. He clicked the mouse another two times.

"Here you go." Duncan pressed play and the screen showed a grainy image of the street and sidewalk in front of the store. One or two people walked past. A couple kissed and held hands as they walked. The street was empty for a while. Then Lacy walked across the screen. I could see myself toddle behind her in the hotdog suit. Again, the street scene seemed quiet. Three or four female tourists walked pass, but in the back of the group was one wearing a hoodie with a frayed sleeve.

"There! Can you pause it?" I asked excitedly, pushing my face closer to the screen. Jason leaned in too, pushing in front to see.

"What are we looking at?" Duncan asked from behind the two of us. He tried to look over my shoulder, tapping on Jason's shoulder.

"Look, the person in the hoodie! That's the person who attacked Lacy! It has to be." I strained to make out more detail in the picture. As I looked more closely, I realized that I couldn't really tell all that much. Certainly, the man in the hoodie wasn't quite as menacing as he'd seemed that evening.

"Hmm…So some guy in a hoodie? I'm not sure that's much help," Jason spoke and leaned on the desk, knocking a stack of papers off. He reached down to pick them up and knocked off another stack. While Jason gathered the papers, he continued: "What have we really got here? Individual in a hoodie, maybe 5 feet five inches, not too tall actually. Probably under 150 pounds." Jason stopped what he was doing and stood up again. He peered at the screen. "Kind of smallish," he said thoughtfully.

"What did you say?" I asked. Had he just described the elf director? That was how I would have described him.

"Looks kind of small," Jason spoke again. He took out his cellphone and dialed someone. He stepped into the other room.

"Man, those women were lucky! They could have been attacked too. I'm surprised they let him walk with them. Yikes!" Duncan said as he looked at the screen. He pulled his glasses from his pocket and put them on, inspecting the screen.

"Thanks, Duncan!" I smiled at him. I walked into the front of the store to look for Jason. He hung up and turned around and looked at me.

"There's something odd about this. I can't put my finger on it, but I think that video will definitely help us narrow down Lacy's boyfriend. We can check it against the video at Bad Daddy's." Jason was already working the details out in his mind.

"Or, you can just ask me who her boyfriend is." I stood straight and tall. Jason stepped towards me and cocked his head to the side.

"Who is her boyfriend?" Jason asked.

"I'm pretty sure her boyfriend is the director Michael Murphy." I smiled triumphantly! I think I had found Lacy's attacker and it could not have been a more annoying guy.

"How do you know that? Did she tell you that?" he pressed.

"She didn't tell me, but her necklace told me. It's a one of a kind, or rather Michael Murphy's wife thinks it's one of kind, but it seems like he might have had a few extras made to give away—if you know what I mean." I winked my eye.

"Is something wrong with your eye?" Jason asked with concern.

"No, I'm saying that I've seen that necklace on his wife and maybe another woman. He probably gives it to his girlfriends," I answered. Jason smirked at me. I thought about what I'd just said and then I caught the double meaning. I crossed my arms and shook my head in disgust at his adolescent humor.

"You should probably call Detective Antoine," Jason suggested. I said goodbye to Duncan, confirming that I had his number if I needed it. He gently closed the glass door behind Jason and me.

Jason and I started our trek to his motorcycle and my car in the garage. This time he walked next to me. He was quiet. I tried to fill the silence with chatter about different things going on around us. As we got closer to the garage, he stopped talking completely. I couldn't stand it.

"Jason, I need to know what's going on." I stopped and gently grabbed his arm. He looked down at my hand. I immediately took it away. His eyes drifted up to my eyes. I returned his gaze.

Finally, he moved, scratching his chin. He turned and started to walk again. I followed him. He took the steps in the garage two at a time, but I kept pace. "Jason, can you just wait a second?"

He reached the top of the stairs and stopped in the doorway. He slipped his hands in his back pockets and lifted his chin, his eyes fixing on some point on the ceiling of the garage. I stood right next to him and pulled on his sleeve.

"You showed up on my date. You kissed me. Now, you aren't going to say anything? Look, you're really cool. I know that. I might not be the coolest person. Maybe you do that all the time, but I don't understand." I placed my hands on my hips and stared him down. He looked down at me.

"I don't understand it either. I, uh..." He took hold of my hands. "I didn't expect that I would..." He stuttered and stopped. He pulled me closer to him. I could smell his scent of leather and something woodsy. His phone rang. He dropped my hands and turned around, taking the call. Saved by the bell, I guess.

Chapter 24

I sat in my car. I could still feel Jason's hands on
mine. I wished he would always hold my hand. I shook
myself from fantasy and dialed Detective Antoine's
number. After two rings, a sing-songy voice answered.
"Hello, this is Donna."

"Is this Detective Antoine?" I asked, unsure if I'd
dialed correctly.

"Yes, of course, who's this?" She immediately
became all business.

"This is Denise Reed. We spoke about a week or two
ago. My friend was attacked on Dauphine Street." I
listened for her reply. I could tell she was thinking
about what I'd said and trying to place what I was
talking about. "I was dressed as a hotdog and my friend
is Lacy Phillips. She works at Bad Daddy's."

"Yes, the hotdog." Her memory was refreshed. I
slumped in my seat. My legacy is to be remembered as
a New Orleans Lucky Dog. "How can I help you, Ms.
Reed?"

"I think that I have a break in the case. I know who
Lacy's boyfriend is. I think he's the one who attacked
her that night." I was excited.

"You have a break in the case?" she asked. I
imagined her raising an eyebrow at me. "You know that
you should leave investigating to the police, don't you,
Ms. Reed?"

"Yes, I know, but I found out who Lacy's boyfriend
is and he must be the one!" I wanted to tell Detective

Antoine and she was slowing me down! I was ready to explode.

"Okay, who's her boyfriend?" Detective Antoine did not sound nearly as impressed as I thought she should be, but I ignored it.

"Her boyfriend is or rather was Michael Murphy, the director!" I shouted into the phone. "It fits! It has to be him. He's small and elf-like. I even saw the security footage at Valmont's Antiques and the guy in the hoodie is on it!"

Detective Antoine was quiet for a while. She sounded like she was pushing air through her teeth, almost shushing me. "She told you he was her boyfriend? He's famous." She was skeptical.

"I know he's famous. No, she didn't tell me it was him, but Lacy has the same necklace as his wife! He probably was trying to get her to back off and she wouldn't so he attacked her!" I put the pieces together perfectly.

"Hold on there, Jessica Fletcher! Just because she has a necklace, doesn't mean the two even know each other. It might just be a popular type of necklace?" Wow! Jessica Fletcher, really? Ouch!

"I think you should at least ask him. Would you please check? I'm sure that I'm right," I pleaded with Detective Antoine. I waited, hoped she would listen to me.

"Okay. I'll look into this. Thank you for telling me. Now, you need to step aside and let the police handle this, okay? Have a good afternoon." I released a sigh of relief as she hung up.

Chapter 25

This day was turning out to be a good one. I'd had an excellent job interview. I'd returned a lost necklace. I'd called Detective Antoine with my suspicions and she hadn't dismissed me. I was pretty sure that I'd solved a mystery. Life was looking up. All I needed to do was wait for the evening news or TMZ to hear the dramatic announcement of the arrest of Lacy's attacker.

I imagined Michael Murphy being pulled from a police car in front of all the cameras, his tiny little wrists actually held by paperclips instead of handcuffs. The mayor would shake my hand, give me a key to the city and all potholes would be filled in my honor!

I decided that this evening I would celebrate. I stopped by the Winn Dixie and picked up all the preparations for supper. I called my mother to inform her that I would cook and to be home promptly by 5 p.m. to watch the news with me. I even picked Emily up early to help me prepare the celebratory meal.

My mother arrived home about 4:58, with a stack of books in hand and entered the kitchen. Emily stood on a stool next to the counter, tearing lettuce and putting it in a wooden bowl for a salad. I chopped garlic, onions and celery to add to my baking dish. My mother said something, but I couldn't hear her.

Finally, I walked into the living room and turned down the television. I wiped my hands on my apron and asked my mom, "What did you say?"

"I said, 'Why is the television on full blast?'" she asked sweetly. She placed her books on the table next to the couch and walked back to the kitchen. I adjusted the volume slightly below deafening and followed her.

"I want to hear the news. I think they'll report something about who attacked Lacy," I said excitedly. I picked up my knife and returned to chopping.

"That's good, but why would you think they know anything?" my mother asked. I could hear a tone of suspicion. She stepped right next to me as I chopped. She leaned closer, inspecting my face. Finally, I put down the knife and looked at her.

"Because I solved the mystery. I figured out who Lacy's boyfriend is or was." I beamed with pride. My mother's expression didn't change. She placed her hands on her hips and tapped a Ked-clad foot, waiting for an explanation.

"Okay, I found Lacy's necklace in my car. I recognized it as the same design that Michael Murphy had given to his wife. Turns out that she even designed it. Lacy all but admitted he was her boyfriend. Or at least Mr. Gicardo at Big Daddy's did," I answered hurriedly and returned to chopping or rather, pulverizing my vegetables. I scooped the veggies off the cutting board and tossed them in the baking dish with the chicken.

"Uh huh, you went to where that girl works?" my mother asked. I could hear her sucking air in through her nose. Somehow she was not as enthusiastic about this as I was.

"Yes, but I took Jason Stone with me." My mom opened her mouth to speak and then closed it. I could tell she was counting in her head. Her eyes glanced over at Emily.

"That could have been very dangerous. I've seen that end of Bourbon Street. Even during the day the place is shady. What makes you so sure that he's her boyfriend?" my mother spoke quietly, trying not to catch Emily's attention.

I looked over to Emily. The bowl was filled with tiny shreds of lettuce. At least we wouldn't need to chew our salads. I handed her another chunk of lettuce. I waved my mother into the living room.

"It has to be this guy. Mr. Gicardo even described him as a snobby shrimp. Michael Murphy *is* a snobby shrimp. Jason and I also went to Duncan Valmont's store on Bienville and looked at the security tapes. You can see a small guy, wearing the same hoodie I saw, following a group of tourists right before the attack," I explained excitedly but quietly. I looked into the kitchen. Emily was still at work.

"Okay, but if he's her boyfriend, why did he attack her? What was the point?" my mother asked. Right there she stumped me. What was the point?

"I don't know," I answered. Right then, the news started. I immediately picked up the remote and turned it up. The first story was something about the Saints. The second was about a mayoral forum on air bed and breakfasts. I waited. My mom looked at the screen and then walked into the kitchen.

I could hear her moving things around. I joined my mother and Emily. My mom popped the chicken into the oven and then began to slice and butter the French bread. "Wait, I was going to make dinner!" I insisted.

"Fine, you slice and I'll butter!" I stood next to Mom and started my slicing. I got quiet. "You're too quiet. What is it, Denise?"

I stopped slicing and looked at her. "Well, I'm positive that Michael Murphy is or was Lacy's boyfriend. How come there hasn't been any mention about the attack on the news? I am, or at least I was, pretty sure he must have been responsible for the attack, but now I'm not sure." My mother nodded and then returned to her buttering.

"Maybe he has powerful lawyers and they're keeping it all hush hush?" my mother speculated. I shrugged. Perhaps she was right. Still, I really wanted to be sure.

"I think that I'll call Detective Antoine and ask." I started to leave the kitchen, when my mother grabbed my arm.

"Didn't you want to tell me about something else?" My mother looked hopeful. I had mentioned that I'd had the interview, but I'd not had a chance to tell her about it. I was still processing the interview.

"I think that the interview went well, but I did knock over a glass of water, almost started crying and I told Rev. Kent about what happened at my old job." As I spoke the words, my heart sank. While I thought the interview felt good, I realized right now how it sounded. I sounded insane.

My mom stopped cutting the bread and yanked me into her arms. She squeezed me tightly. "Hey, what about me?" I felt a tug at my side. Emily looked up at my mother and me and opened her arms wide and wrapped them around my mother and my hips. We all started laughing.

"Mom, I know it sounds really bad, but I actually felt pretty good about the experience." I slipped out of the hug. My mother wrinkled her forehead as she looked at me.

"Denise, I know that someone will see just how wonderful you are and all that you can do! Give it time." She squeezed my arm and returned to the bread.

That evening we feasted on delicious baked chicken, shredded salad, and French bread. We chatted happily during dinner, but doubts crept into my mind. Had Michael Murphy attacked Lacy?

After I put Emily to bed at eight and my mother headed to her room to read, Brock called. "Hey, Denise, it's Brock." He sounded like he was smiling.

"Hi, Brock, how are you?" I asked. I thought back to the text he'd sent only a few days before. I'd totally forgotten to respond. "Oh my goodness, you sent me text and I didn't respond. I'm sorry."

"Oh, it's okay, Denise. I figured that Saturday night was a little weird when Jason showed up. I don't know what that was about." He laughed lightly. I thought about Jason plopping down with us at dinner. "I asked him about it and he said he didn't realize it was a date. Can you believe that guy?"

"No, I really cannot believe him," I said in a monotone. I imagined Jason explaining himself to his co-worker. He said that he didn't realize I was on a date, really?

"He said that he didn't know that you dated," Brock continued to explain. I thought about possibly smothering myself with a pillow. No, the next time I saw Jason, I would smother him with a pillow. "That isn't true, right? You knew it was a date, right?" Brock asked nervously.

"Yes, I knew we were on a date," I answered.

"Because I don't want to bother you or anything, but I had a really good time, up until Jason showed up." He rattled on. I murmured my agreement. I, too, had really enjoyed the date, up until Jason showed up. Strangely, until that point in the date, I'd been wondering about what it would have been like if Brock kissed me or if there would be a second date. When Jason appeared, though, all I thought about was him. Frankly, he was all I could think about for the last few days.

"So, do you want to go out again?" he asked breathlessly. My mind returned to the conversation at hand.

"Sure, but when were you thinking?" I asked. I wasn't sure. He gave me a date and time. I looked towards Emily's room and thought for a moment. "Let me work on getting a sitter and I'll get back to you. Is that okay?"

"That sounds great. Good night, Denise." Again, before I could even finish saying 'goodnight,' Brock hung up. I held the phone to my chest. I needed some sort of clarity and everything felt as clear as mud.

I parked myself on the couch and turned on the television, trying to lose myself in some stupid sitcom. I watched the news again at ten and still there was no mention of the attack on Lacy. I thought I might try to stay up and watch TMZ, but I was too tired and went to bed.

Chapter 26

My phone rang early in the morning. I looked at the number, a California area code. I picked up.

"Hello, is this Denise?" a painfully cheerful voice asked. I cleared my voice and looked down at my watch. It was 6:30 a.m. Who calls at 6:30 a.m.?

"Yes, this is Denise," I answered.

"Hello, this is Nancy from Golden Shore Productions?" I was pretty sure she wasn't asking a question, but she ended every sentence like she asking a question. "We were wondering if you were available today to be an extra? We know this is short notice? So we'll actually pay you $100 if you'd be able to work today for about four hours this morning at Audubon Park?" I couldn't tell which was actually a question.

I thought about telling her no. I was tired of the movie business, but I was also curious. Had the police arrested Michael Murphy? I saw nothing on the news last night. I also still wasn't working. "Uh, okay. What time would you like me to be there? And where?" I wondered if I'd be dressed as a hotdog again.

Chapter 27

I dropped Emily off at pre-school and headed back towards Audubon Park. The movie shoot was set next to the fountain across from Tulane University on St. Charles' Avenue. I found a parking spot on Calhoun Street and trekked down Coralie Street into the park. Today the weather had finally changed. It was getting cooler.

Despite the early hour, the park was active. Folks jogged down the main pathway. Bicyclists pedaled quickly around the path. There was a Tai-Chi group on a grassy field exercising. The new chill in the air had brought everyone out this morning.

I buttoned my sweater and made my way to the set. The crew milled around, sipping their coffee and checking in on their headsets. I finally located Nancy and checked in.

"Hello, Nancy, I'm Denise Reed." She didn't look up from her clipboard. She flipped furiously through the pages.

"Francis, come in, Francis. We have a problem." She spoke into her head set. The other person responded, "Look, this scene requires Ellis in it, but he's still out with mono...I don't know maybe he'll be in a little later, but I need someone now..." She listened for a beat and finally looked up at me. She lifted one finger at me. I couldn't hear the response, but she continued, "Well, how am I supposed to do that? Fine. Fine!"

She smiled at me sweetly. "How can I help you?" I smiled back.

"I'm here as an extra. You called me this morning. My name is Denise Reed." She looked at me thoughtfully. She was trying to place me. She tapped her finger on her cheek.

"You dressed as the hotdog, didn't you?" She snapped her fingers. I nodded. She nodded. "Hold on a sec." She pressed the side of headset and started speaking again. "Francis, I think I have someone who can do Ellis' part." She listened and said "uh-huh" a few times. "I'll get her to fill out a release."

She looked back at me and straightened her headset, "Denise, would you be willing to be in this scene with Chase Clarke?" Now, I knew that Nancy had just said something about filling out a release. I also know that usually if you have to fill out a release, it means they want you to release them—the movie production company—from liability. This was probably a bad idea or at least something that might result in injury. I pressed my lips together. I tried to control myself. "We'll throw in another $100?"

What can I say? I would be in a scene with Chase Clarke. "What would this scene entail?" I asked.

Chapter 28

Twenty minutes later, I was sitting on the edge of the fountain. I was dressed in a spit-up green housecoat, an oversized torn men's tweed jacket, a yellow knit scarf, and a dirty fedora covering my hair stuffed into a shower cap. A grocery cart was directly to my left, filled with newspapers, aluminum cans and items meant to be knocked over and scattered.

I looked at the other extras. There was a gentleman to my right dressed as a street musician. He strummed lightly on his guitar. I was not sure if he was really in costume. To my left there was a guy dressed as a mime in full white make-up. At least this day my costume was not that bad.

Claudia crossed the set and approached me. She cleared her throat and I looked up at her. She blinked.

"Oh, it's you again. The hotdog!" Somehow she didn't say that with affection.

"Yes, I'm the hotdog," I answered flatly. I looked around the crew. I hadn't seen the director yet. Had he already been arrested? I was ripped from my thoughts when Claudia gripped my chin in her hand and turned my head to look at her. She reached into her back pocket and pulled out a giant mascara. She opened it and dabbed the wand on both my cheeks. She then spread the black marks on my cheeks.

Claudia pushed a button on the side of her headset and murmured into it. She smiled at me, but the smile somehow didn't reach her eyes. "I'm so glad you're back." Let's just say, she was not going to win an

Academy Award for acting. "Okay, I'm going to need you to stand there and look at the fountain. Chase is going to push you to one side and he's going to send this grocery cart flying." With that, she turned on her heels and clicked away.

Despite it being cooler, all the layers were getting warm. I looked toward the trailer, waiting. Would Michael Murphy be here? I wondered when I would see Chase Clarke.

At last, the door of one of the trailers opened. Michael Murphy emerged with his wife right behind him. He gingerly helped her down the steps. Again, members of the crew fluttered around her like moths to a light bulb. Her smile was radiant.

She began her procession around the set. She shook hands, shared a laugh and smile. She made her way closer to me, and I could see that once again she was wearing her beloved, "one of a kind," necklace. It glistened on her thin neck.

She clapped her hands and someone handed her a bullhorn. "I just want to thank you all for welcoming me, your producer, to the set. I cannot wait to see this scene. I'm so proud of your work and my husband assures me that this will be the final week of shooting. You'll be seeing a lot of me for the rest of the shoot." A couple of the crew laughed and she raised a perfectly drawn eyebrow at her husband. He smiled weakly and shrugged. She handed off the bullhorn and someone shouted "Places!".

I turned toward the fountain and looked at the water, waiting for a shove from Chase Clarke. I heard the director shout: "Action!" I rocked back and forth and waited. I heard the sound of footsteps on the pavement thundering toward me. I turned just a shade to see that glorious hunk of man barreling toward me, and instinctively I stepped backwards to my right. His eyes grew large and his mouth opened in horror as he missed me and flew over the side of the fountain and landed in the water.

"Cut! What the hell was that?" shouted the director. He threw down his clipboard. Immediately folks ran to the fountain. Chase Clarke stood up in the fountain. His expression was shocked as he looked down at himself. I had to admit that even soaking wet muscle looked pretty good.

Claudia and Mrs. Murphy both ran to the fountain, reaching toward Chase. The two took hold of his muscular arms and assisted him over the side of the fountain. Chase just started muttering. I couldn't quite make out what he was saying but it might have been: "It wasn't supposed to be me. She was supposed to fall in." He looked between the two women with utter bewilderment.

Mrs. Murphy looked over at Claudia, "Claudia would you be a dear and go grab Chase a coffee and a blank—" She stopped midsentence and let go of Chase's arm and stepped toward Claudia. Her eyes crept down Claudia's face to Claudia's neck, landing on the necklace. The color drained from Mrs. Murphy's face.

She marched over to the director, and it was obvious what would happen next. The question was would we all witness it? She gripped her husband on the shoulder and glared down at him. Without a word, he squirmed from his director's chair and followed his wife to the trailer.

I looked back at Chase Clarke. He was still wide-eyed and unsure. Finally he sputtered out: "But I was supposed to knock you into the water!" I rolled my eyes. Looking at him made me shiver so I pulled the coat closed.

"Does my hair look okay?" he asked sadly. I shrugged my shoulders. What could I tell him? The front part was sticking straight up and another part was plastered to one side of his face. He reached up to feel and I think that I saw his hair shift as a whole unit. Wait, it was a wig?

I looked toward Claudia as she stomped away. Another crew member stopped her and she shooed him away. He held a hoodie in his hand and ran toward Chase and handed it to him. Something about the jacket looked familiar.

Before he could slip the jacket on, I stepped closer and grabbed its sleeve. The cuff was frayed and torn. I dropped it immediately and stared at the actor.

"Is this your jacket?" I asked quietly.

"Nah, mine's leather, but I don't want to ruin it, you know?" he said matter of factly and pulled off his shirt exposing his glorious torso. I only ogled a little bit until I tore my eyes away. I heard the zip of the jacket and looked back.

Clearly it was not his jacket because he was bulging in it. His arms were at least two inched longer than the sleeves. Still, it was someone on the set's jacket.

"Is that the director's jacket?" I asked, but Chase was already walking towards his trailer, peeling off his other clothing as he went. I was mesmerized. Again, he tapped down the hair on the back of his head. Yep, it had to be a toupee.

The crew milled around and we waited. I wandered from my position and moved closer to the trailers. I could hear glass shattering and shouting from the director's trailer. I was almost feeling sorry for the grouchy elf.

Once again, I know that eavesdropping is wrong, but can I help it if a snack table was located so near to the trailer and they were shouting? Yes, I know that I can, but I didn't stop myself. I found a bag of barbecue potato chips and ripped them open, eating and listening to the exchange.

"I cannot believe you! How long has this been going on?" a voice demanded. The response was muffled. "What? I don't know what I'm talking about? I'm crazy?" With that, another sound of shattering glass came from the trailer.

"If some random extra noticed, then everyone must know! Don't you dare deny it!" Again I could hear only a muffled response and then another sound of breaking furniture. With that, the door flew open and Michael Murphy tumbled down the steps. His eyes landed on me and they froze.

He stepped towards me. Shaking a finger at me, he shouted: "How did you know? This is your fault!" He started to chase me around the snack table. The rest of the crew stood frozen in their spots, watching me bob and weave around the table, throwing snacks as I ran.

"I'm not the one who was doing something wrong! This is your own fault. At least find some other trinket to give your girlfriends. You were too obvious!" I stood my ground on one side of the table. I could hear a gasp from behind me. Murphy lunged across the table, falling short and landing on a fruit tray. He stood up and was about to say something to me except a book flew at him from the doorway of the trailer and hit him square between his eyes. He immediately hit the pavement.

A wild-eyed Nadine Murphy peeked her head out the door. She pointed at one of the members of the crew. The man looked terrified as he pointed at himself, confirming that he'd been chosen. "You! Go get Claudia!" she demanded. She walked down the short steps and stood over Michael Murphy. He curled into a ball. "You get back in here!" she spoke through gritted teeth.

"She's right next to the trailer," the frightened crewman answered, pointing to Claudia. Claudia was hiding next to the trailer, obviously hoping Nadine wouldn't see her. Claudia's glare shot daggers at the crewman for outing her. Nadine turned slowly, her eyes falling on Claudia. She crooked her finger at Claudia, beckoning her to the trailer.

I took that as my cue. I decided that now would be a good time to go somewhere else. In fact, it would probably have been the best time to head to the library and keep working on my resume. I thought it might be a good idea to leave my show business credits off my CV. Frankly, I'm not sure how I would phrase it. Maybe: "Accidently exposes extra-marital affairs of famous directors."

I returned to the costume trailer and changed. Even from there, I could hear shouts and accusations from the other trailer. I folded up my costume and headed to the woman in charge of wardrobe. A breathless man walked up to the table.

Something about him was familiar. He was a little taller than me. His hair was the same shade as mine. No hips. "You must be, Ellis?" He nodded at me and I handed him the costume.

I heard a member of the crew make an announcement. The shoot was shut down "temporarily." I had a feeling that this Chase Clarke action comedy would never see the light of day. Of course, what was going on behind the scenes was much more exciting. It was a shame. I guess no one would get to appreciate my skills as an actress. That might have been for the best.

Fifteen minutes later, I began my walk to my car. The park was a little less full now that it had been at 10 a.m. The sun was shining and it felt good, but suddenly I felt the hair on the back of neck stand up. I stopped and looked around me.

All I saw were a couple of joggers. In the distance, I saw folks from the movie packing up and heading towards their cars. I tried to shake the feeling of being watched, but I couldn't.

I walked quickly and headed for Coralie Street. I stopped again and turned. Again, nothing out of the ordinary in the park caught my attention. A bicyclist pedaled past. I heard a shout from the field as two men threw a Frisbee back and forth.

I pulled my purse closer and moved faster. I was coming to some denser oak trees and the entrance to Coralie Street. Again I stopped and turned. This time I saw something or someone. They shouldn't have seemed out of place, just a lone jogger in sweats, but the hood was up and I couldn't see their face. Could that have been the same hoodie from the night of the attack?

I wasn't going to stay there and find out. I started running to my car. I reached into my purse and pulled out my keys, clicking the unlock button. I skidded to a stop at the car and yanked the door open. I hopped in and slammed the door shut, panting and trying to catch my breath. That was it! I needed to do more cardio!

I put the key in the ignition and looked out my windshield. I could see the jogger coming. I started the car and began to back up. Whoever it was, they stopped and turned around. I backed into someone's driveway and headed towards Calhoun Street. I took a right and sped home.

I made it back to Mom's house in record time and in fact found a parking place on Joseph Street, almost in front of the house. As I got out, I scanned my surroundings. Everything seemed normal, just folks parking and going to the Whole Foods on Magazine Street, maybe a mother pushing her child in a stroller.

I finally got out of the car and headed to the house. I unlocked the door, walked in and immediately locked it behind me. I ran to my room and closed the door. I pulled out my phone and dialed Detective Antoine's number. She answered on the second ring.

"Hello, this is Detective Antoine," A cheerful voice answered. She sounded so sweet, but I knew that sweetness disguised the tenacity of a bulldog on a bone.

"Hello, Detective Antoine, this is Denise Reed. We spoke about Michael Murphy yesterday. I think that he was following me a little while ago," I blurted out.

"Wait, what?" She was not following what I was talking about. "Ms. Reed, would you please start at the beginning?"

"Okay, this is Denise Reed. I was with Lacy Phillips when she was attacked a couple of weeks ago. You and I spoke after it happened?" I reminded her and waited.

"You were dressed as a hotdog?" she asked.

"Yes. I was the hotdog. I called you yesterday that I found out who her boyfriend was. He gave her the necklace that he also gave to his wife, Michael Murphy?" Again I waited to hear her response. I started pacing my room.

"You mean Lacy Phillip's boyfriend or ex-boyfriend?" she clarified, "You said that she was dating Michael Murphy, the director of the new Chase Clarke movie."

"Yes, I told you because I think or thought that he attacked her that night," I reminded her. I was growing inpatient.

"He didn't do it." she answered. "He has the alibi of about 50 witnesses."

"That cannot be right. He gave her that necklace. He's her boyfriend." I was incredulous. I sat on my bed and slumped.

"I didn't say that he wasn't her boyfriend, but he did not attack her. There is actual video of him screaming at members of his crew, demanding his assistant. I can't blame her for hiding from him. It probably went on for about 15 minutes until the girl finally arrived. The video is time stamped. You didn't see it last night on TMZ?" she asked me. "What were you saying about him following you?"

"I thought he was following me in the park," I answered. I guess it wasn't him, but it was someone in that same sweatshirt. Who was it?

"Are you in a safe place?" she asked seriously. I looked around my room for anything resembling a weapon. I noticed a Fisher-Price popcorn popper toy. I picked it up.

"I'm at home," I answered, weapon in hand.

"If you think that you're in danger, you need to hang up with me and call the police right now," she spoke firmly.

"Okay, I'll call the police." I hung up the phone and let out a breath I was holding. How was it possible that Michael Murphy had not attacked Lacy? I thought about what Detective Antoine had said about the TMZ video.

I wandered to the kitchen and turned on my laptop. I clicked on the TMZ website. Admittedly, this must have been a busy day for celebrity disasters. I found the video that Detective Antoine had spoken about. I clicked the link and waited.

The video was from someone's phone. The first part of the video showed the director silently fuming as he walked next to a trailer, tapping his clipboard on his leg. He cocked his head to one side and nodded at someone who was off camera. Two crewmen came over and then the tirade began.

I turned down the volume on the computer. His screed was a profanity-filled tirade about the lighting having the wrong gel, something about angle of the camera (but that part was the most bleeped out) and finally about what he planned to do to that bleepity-bleep hotdog bleep. He slammed his clipboard on the ground and seemed to calm down momentarily. It appeared he realized that he had a shell-shocked audience. He then looked down at the clipboard.

"Where's Claudia?" he asked to no one in particular. No one answered. Again, he asked even louder, this time kicking the clipboard. At that point, the video ended. In the corner of the video was indeed the time stamp. Michael Murphy may have been a super jerk, but he couldn't have been at two places at one time.

I paced the kitchen, rolling the popcorn popper behind me. I walked back to my room. I picked up my phone.

So, I was back to wondering: who had been following me in the park? Perhaps I should've dialed 911? I even started to dial 911, but I felt like maybe I was being hysterical. Maybe someone was not following me. People wear sweat shirts to run. I tried to convince myself, but I couldn't. Instead I dialed Jason's number.

"This is Stone," Jason answered on the first ring.

"Hi, it's Denise. Uh, I think someone was following me in the park. I'm feeling pretty freaked out," I blurted out.

"Have you called 911?" Jason asked immediately.

"I thought that maybe I was being ridiculous," I mumbled into the phone. "I'm home now." I heard him sigh.

"Denise, if you think you might be in danger, you should call the police," he scolded. I hung my head and nodded, as if he could have seen me.

"The thing is I was at Audubon Park for the movie shoot and then they cancelled it. I thought someone wearing that hoodie was following me," I explained.

Jason listened silently. I waited for him to respond. For a moment I thought perhaps he'd hung up. "You saw that same hoodie again?"

"Yes, actually, I think I saw it twice. First someone gave it to Chase Clarke after he fell in the fountain. Then I think I saw a jogger wearing it," I told him.

"Chase Clarke was wearing this hoodie or could it have been a jacket that looked like it?" He was skeptical.

"Well, first he fell in the fountain. When they were helping him out, a crew member handed him the jacket and he put it on, but it didn't really fit. It was way too small, but it was the same sweatshirt. The sleeve was frayed," I explained, thinking back on what I'd observed. Chase Clarke's muscles were bulging in that sweatshirt. I thought I would leave that part out when talking to Jason.

All I heard was a "hmm" on the other end of the phone. I couldn't interpret what he was thinking.

"I tell you what, Denise, I'm going to come over for a little bit, okay? I'm only about ten minutes away. Hang tight." He hung up. I perched on the edge of my bed, gripping my Fisher-Price popcorn popper weapon.

After a few minutes, the urge to pee was overpowering. I laid down my arms and ran to the bathroom. Feeling refreshed, I noticed just how hungry I felt. I started to relax and decided that perhaps a peanut butter and jelly sandwich was in order. While I was at it, maybe I'd watch another video on TMZ's website.

Still a little early for lunch, but a snack wouldn't hurt, so I went into the kitchen in search of peanut butter. No sooner had I took the peanut butter from the cabinet, than my phone rang. I walked back into my bedroom. The number was local but I didn't recognize it. I went ahead and picked up.

"Hello, this is Denise," I answered.

"Hello Denise, this is Rev. Kent from St. Basil's Church." I recognized his voice immediately. "I was wondering if we could talk for a moment." I could almost hear the smile in his voice. At least, I hoped it was a smile.

"Yes, of course, Rev. Kent. I can talk," I answered hopefully. My chest was swelling with excitement. Was this it? Could this be it?

I jumped up and down in my room, trying to release some of this energy and excitement. I waited expectantly for his words. He cleared his throat. I waited. I sat, but then decided against sitting. I was too excited, but now I was breathing a little heavy.

I again headed for the kitchen and attempted to control my breathing. I could hear someone rustling at the door. I figured it was probably my mother coming home for lunch after her volunteering in the morning. Usually when my mother came home, she would announce herself. She was going to be so excited too!

"Denise, I'd like to offer you a position at St. Basil's as our new outreach coordinator. I think that you would be perfect for this. What do you say?" These were the words I'd hoped to hear for the last six months. I wanted to shout yippee and slug down a bottle of champagne!

"Yes!" I practically shouted into the phone. No sense in being coy with the man. I couldn't wait to tell my mom when she walked in.

I ran to the front door just as the lock clicked. I was about to swing the door open, but I stopped abruptly. The door inched open. I stepped backwards. The door opened all the way.

It took a moment for me to register what was happening. Somehow I kept expecting my mother to be standing in the doorway, but this was not my mother. Clad in skinny jeans, a V-neck sweater and a hoodie—the hoodie—stood Claudia.

I froze to my spot and listened as Rev. Kent chatted. My throat was dry and I could feel sweat under my arms. I was terrified. Rev. Kent thanked me and said his goodbye. I stepped backwards towards the dining room and dropped my phone.

She stepped closer to me and stopped. "Hi, Denise, I just wanted to come by and talk with you. Is that okay?" Her tone was sweet. She smiled behind her tiny glasses, but I saw that she held one hand behind her back.

The hair on my scalp and arms stood straight up. I swallowed and tried to stay calm as my heart pounded in my chest. I thought anyone could hear it. Why, for the love of all things good, had I put down my popcorn popper? Where had I put down my popcorn popper?

I cleared my throat and pasted a smile on my face. "What are you doing here, Claudia?" I'm not sure why I even bothered to ask. I knew what she was doing here.

"You knew Michael and I were together and you had to tell her." Claudia took a step closer to me. I took a step back.

"Yes, I knew that you were having an affair with Michael Murphy, as did anyone else with eyes, but I did not tell Nadine Murphy," I responded. "For that matter, it looked like he was having quite a few affairs."

Claudia clucked her tongue and tapped one foot, "No, they were nothing to him. Those were just some stupid flings and I took care of them. He loves me."

"Them?" I asked. I scanned the room for some sort of weapon. She positioned herself between me and the door.

"Lois and Colleen." She rolled her eyes. I thought back to the story I'd overheard on the set. The two crewmen called the movie "cursed." She continued, "They figured it out real quick that they needed to leave Michael alone. Lacy was too stupid to take a hint. She thought she was special. She needed more persuasion." I had a feeling that "persuasion" was in Claudia's hand, behind her back.

"So, you were jealous that that cheater gave Lacy a necklace too, just like you?" I wanted to keep her talking. Jason was coming over. For that matter, my mother would be home soon too. Again, she stepped closer to me. I would move towards one side and she would mirror my moves.

"I'm the special one." She spoke in a whisper and lowered her head, glowering at me. I didn't want to anger her. I needed to keep her talking, distract her so I could run.

"So, you followed us that night?" I offered and waited for Claudia's reply.

"I saw you two walk away from the set. I followed you. You didn't even notice me." She shook her head when she said it. I remembered back to the tape. Duncan had mentioned how strange it was that the group of women tourists behind us didn't seem to notice the person in the hoodie behind them. Of course, Claudia would have fit right in to a group of women. Who would have realized what a threat she actually was?

"You stabbed Lacy because Michael Murphy had started to see her. You wanted her to leave him and she wouldn't listen." I moved to the left and she leaned in that direction. I moved to the right. "Yeah, you were special all right. Just like all the others, but not anymore, right?" I just wanted to keep her talking while I tried to move toward the door. She stepped backwards, reaching behind her and pushing the door completely closed.

"No!" she shouted. One of her hands flailed out in front of her, as if she could stop my words with her hand.

She crossed the space between us in an instant. Her hand came from behind her back and I recognized the glint of metal as she slashed it at me. I instantly twisted, barely missing the blade. I turned fully and tried to run towards the kitchen. The telephone sat idly on the counter.

I felt the pull and needles of pain pricked my scalp. Claudia had grabbed my hair and pulled back my head. Her other hand was poised ready with the knife to slit across my throat. I reached out for anything to try to pull away. At last, my hand grabbed the arm of a dining room table chair. I yanked the chair behind me.

I heard Claudia grunt. Her grip loosened and I yanked my head forward and pulled away, rushing into the kitchen. She charged at me slashing and grabbing as I tried to dodge her. The razor sharp blade nicked my arm. I let out a scream.

I looked desperately around the kitchen for something to grab. I saw the Fisher-Price popcorn popper on the kitchen table. I picked it up and hit her with it. She raised her hand to deflect the blows and then knocked it away. It was just making her more angry.

She lunged at me and we both fell to the floor. My popcorn popper slipped from my grip. Her knife clattered on the ground. I saw it under the table and she grabbed it first.

"Do come on in, Jason. I'm sure Denise is right…Oh my gosh—" I heard my mother from the other room. I gripped Claudia's wrist but the knife still moved closer and closer. She slashed it wildly. Again it nicked my hand. I heard my mother's quick steps and Jason pounding behind her.

Before I could even yell, I saw a white Ked kick the side of Claudia's head. Claudia rocked to one side and the same white Ked continued through with another kick. I wiggled out of Claudia's grip and scooted across the floor. In some strange almost ballet move, my mother was now crouched on top of Claudia, one foot on the back of her neck and her knee in the middle of Claudia's back. With one hand, my mother held Claudia's hand in an unnatural twist. She shook Claudia's hand until Claudia dropped the knife. Finally, she grabbed both of Claudia's hands and pinned them under her knee.

"Stay down or I'll put you down!" my mother commanded a whimpering Claudia. Claudia held still. I sat up from my position on the floor. My mouth hung open as I looked at my mother.

My mother was in a perfectly pressed navy sweater set, grey slacks and pearls. She looked like she was about to have a casual lunch with her friends. She was calm and composed.

"Mom?" I asked. She didn't take her eyes off Claudia. Somehow I knew that if Claudia moved, it would have been for the last time in her life. Claudia gurgled from the floor. I looked up at Jason. He looked equally as perplexed.

"Mrs. Reed, I'll go ahead and take it from here. If that's okay with you?" Jason asked respectfully from behind my mother. My mother turned and looked back at Jason and smiled. Claudia let out a little grunt.

Carefully, my mother changed places with Jason. He pulled handcuffs from his pocket and began to read Claudia her rights. My mother watched mesmerized. Finally my mother looked at me. Gently she reached out towards me and pulled me into her arms. From Double 07 to Mommy in 60 seconds. Who knew that my mother was a secret bad ass?

Chapter 29

Finally, things appeared to have settled down. That evening, after the police and EMTs and curious neighbors disappeared, my mother and I sat on the front porch swing in silence. Emily was tucked in bed after a fierce negotiation for one more book and song.

We rocked back and forth. I shifted a bag of ice on my scalp. It was only a little sore now. I examined my hand and arm. Just nicks covered with ointment and Band-Aids. My mother stretched her arms above her head. I watched her, waiting. She patted me on the arm.

"I'm so glad to hear you got the position at St. Basil's Church. How soon can you start?" Her eyes glittered with excitement. Certainly I wanted to talk about my good news, but my mind was still replaying my mom's action star moves. She'd just clobbered a crazed woman threatening her daughter in her kitchen, and she wanted to talk about my new position?

"Okay, Mom, I have to ask this. How did you do that today?" I waited for her answer. She closed her eyes and smiled.

"Yoga and Pilates class?" she answered innocently. I pursed my lips at my mother.

"I don't know what yoga class you've been going to, Mom, but that was not a yoga move." I leaned closer.

"Denise, my dear, some things have to remain a mystery. I hate violence." She laughed. "Besides, you need to tell me what you'll be doing at St. Basil's." She tried to change the subject.

"Come on, Mom!" I poked her on the arm. I didn't want to touch her too hard. What if she practiced one of those moves on me?

"It's from a long time ago. It's funny how some lessons stay with you throughout your whole life," my mother answered mysteriously. This would require some snooping, but not tonight. She pressed her lips together. She was not revealing a thing.

"Okay, Mom, you're off the hook for now, but I will find out. You know that I'm pretty good at figuring out a mystery." We both laughed, rocking the swing, knowing that somehow I would figure out her story, but for tonight we would relish the good news of my gainful employment.

Lying in bed that evening, I prayed in thanksgiving for my life. I smiled under the covers, thinking about a new position. I heard my phone ding with a text. I turned over and picked up the phone.

I read the text. It was from Jason. "I am glad you're okay." Again I smiled.

I texted back: "I am too. Thank you for being there." I sent the text and immediately saw the little dots. He was writing a response.

"Your mom is really cool, but I'm a little intimidated." I smiled at his text. The little dots appeared again.

"I'm sorry I ruined your date with Brock," the next text read. Again the dots. "Don't go out with Brock." Oh, boy, what did that mean? I shifted and sat up.

"Why not?" I typed and waited for his response.

I watched the little dots and waited. What would he write?

"Just don't, okay?" the words pleaded. I thought about pressing him. Maybe I'd tease him that Brock and I were already engaged, but something told me not to do that.

"Okay. I'm not sure that I could get a babysitter on Friday anyway," I wrote back. Again I saw the dots.

"That's good. Good night, Denise." I held the phone to my chest and let my head fall back on the pillow. I put the phone back on the night stand. This was one more mystery I'd have to figure out in the morning. I turned over and fell asleep.

Chapter 30

Early the next morning, I checked my email. I'd received a message from Carolyn at The Education Tree Organization. Despite being a "strong candidate" for the position, they felt my skills did not fit the position. Apparently they'd decided to go with a different candidate and wished me the best of luck. Just getting that email made me feel lucky not to have gotten the job. Of course, I wondered if perhaps they'd found a nice dinosaur for the position.

I dressed quickly, drove Emily to pre-school and again made my way to the Quarter. This time I parked in Canal Place. I made my way down Decatur Street to Jackson Square.

I glanced at my wristwatch. It was almost ten and Café du Monde was already crowded and noisy. This morning a street performer was playing the most mournful saxophone version of "When the Saints Go Marching In" I'd ever heard. On the other side, someone was making animal balloons for children. I weaved through the tables and found one near a column and sat. I scanned the street, waiting for my friends. I rested my arms on the table and immediately lifted them to discover them covered in powdered sugar.

"Hey, Denise!" I turned to find Lacy standing right behind me. I hardly recognized Lacy. This day she was in a tight cream sweater and dark blue jeans with ballet flats. Her brown hair was pulled into a simple ponytail. Her face was clear and bright, not a bit of makeup.

"Hello, Lacy! I'm so glad to see you." She immediately sat down at the table and we ordered our café au lait and beignets with powdered sugar. She sipped her water and leaned back in her chair.

"See, this is the best part, Denise!" She nodded her head knowingly. She stretched her arms behind her, striking a relaxed pose.

"The best part of what?" I asked. I was confused.

"The best part is getting to sit back and watch the world. Look at this place! Ooh, I think that's a clown over there!" I turned to where she pointed. Indeed, someone dressed as Pennywise the Clown was frightening tourists for money. "If you were working or busy, you'd never get to see anything like that."

I agreed. "So true. If I was working today I would have missed that. Or, of course, I could be murdered by a scary clown because I'm not working." We both laughed and tried not to make eye contact with the fellow. The waiter arrived with our order and we paid. I lifted the warm coffee to my lips.

"If you'd been working, you wouldn't have figured out who attacked me and made sure she got arrested." She said the words point blank. I put the coffee mug down. I considered her words.

"You knew it was Claudia the whole time, didn't you?" I watched her response to my words. She didn't deny them.

"I guess that I did, but I wasn't sure at first. That night it was dark and I couldn't see her face." She bit down on her beignet and again leaned back in her chair.

"How did *you* figure it out?" I asked her.

She bit the side of her lip and thought for a moment. Then she sat up straight. "When you brought me my phone and you told me there weren't any calls that night, I knew it. She thought she didn't need to keep harassing me because she'd gotten rid of me." Lacy wiped an invisible tear from the side of her eye. She picked up her cup, blew on the hot liquid and sipped. Her eyes challenged me to ask her why.

I took the challenge: "Why didn't you tell the police?" She sighed deeply and put down her coffee.

"Let me ask you a question, Denise. If you and I hadn't talked and gotten to know each other before I told you what I did for a living, would we even be speaking right now?" Her question was pointed. I reflected on my answer.

How would I have responded if I knew at first that she was a dancer? Would I have dismissed her and not talked to her? Would I have wanted to be her friend? Would I have learned anything else about her life?

"I don't know, Lacy, but I'm glad that we did talk," I answered honestly. I hoped that I wouldn't have pre-judged Lacy, but I might have. "I would like to think it wouldn't have changed anything, but I'm glad I didn't have that choice. I'm glad we're becoming friends." I could tell she was thinking about my answer.

"So, we're friends?" she whispered the question. Her eyes were unsure but hopeful.

"I should say so." I sat up straighter in my chair and raised an eyebrow. She feigned distress slapping her hands to her cheeks.

"Thanks!" Lacy lifted her cup and clinked the side of mine, "Cheers!" We both sipped our coffee.

We sat there drinking our coffee, eating our beignets and watching the world for a little while. Lacy told me her Thanksgiving plans. I told her mine. Again, we compared pictures of our daughters and cooed. She finally sent me the selfie we'd taken the evening of the attack. I told her about finally getting a new position.

"So, I guess I'll need to find another hotdog to hang out with," she said. I smiled at the image. I shrugged. She went on: "because you were really the best; you were a real wiener." We both groaned at the pun. Right about that time, Carrie and Duncan Valmont arrived at Café Du Monde.

The two scanned the café, looking for me. I waved at both of them simultaneously. When they reached the table, both laughed.

"I was wondering who this other person was," Duncan spoke first, his thumb indicating Carrie. I introduced the group to each other. Everyone squeezed around the table and ordered more coffee and beignets.

"Lacy, when we first met, you said that you'd been looking around for more opportunities to 'hone your craft' and it turns out that Duncan and some of his friends have a community theater group. I thought you should meet." The two looked across the table at each other.

"Really, you do theater?" Lacy asked Duncan. He placed his hand over his heart and crossed it. They both laughed and immediately launched into theater chatter.

"I see what you did there." Carrie shook a finger at me. She sipped her coffee. "You're being a friend, helping people. Good work!" She put her arm around my shoulders and hugged.

Lacy glanced over at me. "Oh, by the way, Big T told me to remind you that Book Club is this Thursday. The theme for snacks is Parisian brunch, whatever that means." She smiled at me and I nodded. I guess I was joining a book club with the neon mountain or rather 'Big T.' I'd need to look up "Parisian brunch" before Thursday or else.

Chapter 31

Things were busy over the next couple of days. I headed out to St. Basil's several times to fill out paperwork. Rev. Kent showed me where my office would be. I met the other four people on staff. We all went out for a delicious poor boy lunch at the place on Bonnabel. This time I actually ate my roast beef sandwich with gusto. I'd be starting the week after Thanksgiving.

Later, while perusing TMZ's website I came across a short article about the Michael Murphy film. As it turned out, he was fired as director of the film by the Quinn Company. Turns out, three or four former employees on the film are suing him for sexual harassment. His soon to be ex-wife, former actress, Nadine Quinn, took over the directing of the film and completed it in two weeks. The buzz is that her version has award stamped all over it. The movie is set to be released sometime next fall.

On Thursday evening, I joined Big T, Lacy, Mr. Gicardo, his wife Tania, and a whole host of other interesting characters at CC's on Royal Street to discuss *Messy Spirituality*, eat baby quiches and drink mimosas. The experience was joyful and thought-provoking. Of course, much like Fight Club, what happens at Book Club stays at Book Club. I can tell you that the group decided to take Thanksgiving off, review the proposed books and make their next selection for book club the first week in December. I'm rooting for

Mere Christianity by C.S. Lewis, but most of the group had already read it.

Duncan and Lacy started working on a play almost as soon as we all left our coffee meet. I'd already fielded about fourteen texts a day from each of them wondering if I'd help them gather props for their next production of one-act plays in January. Duncan also wanted to know if I'd make a special cameo as the hotdog in an avant-garde version of Tennessee Williams' *Cat on a Hot Tin Roof.* I said I'd think about it.

I certainly felt I had a lot to be thankful about. I couldn't believe that I was finally returning to full time employment and that my main task would be to help people. I felt good about it. While driving back to the house, my phone rang. I picked up without looking who was calling.

"Hello," I almost sang into the phone.

"Hello to you too, Denise!" I recognized Jason's voice immediately. He sounded like he was smiling. "Why do you sound so happy?" he asked.

"I'm starting my new position a couple of weeks after Thanksgiving. You sound pretty happy too," I answered. I couldn't stop smiling. As I drove along Metairie Road, everything seemed green and rosy. It must have been my mood.

"I was wondering if you would meet me at the little café at City Park, the one near the pavilions with the lions." I knew exactly where he was describing. After confirming where we'd meet, I hung up.

I knew the place. The playground there was amazing. I continued down Metairie Road until it became City Park Avenue. Across from Ralph's on the Park. I turned between the stone pillars that marked one entrance into the oak filled City Park. I crossed the small train tracks and tiny stone bridge and turned right. I pulled my car into a spot across from City Putt.

I saw Jason leaning against the bandstand pavilion, closest to the café. His long legs stretched out in blue jeans and a brown sweater. He looked like he'd fallen off the cover of GQ. He watched me as I approached. His arms were crossed and he shifted his weight slightly. Usually the area was filled with children running around and playing, climbing on the friendly oaks or tossing bread to the huge geese in the lagoon.

Today, at this moment, the park was quiet. A slight breeze blew around the scattered leaves on the ground. The sun was warm, but it wasn't too hot. A large tour bus was just pulling away from the curb. A mother and her child played near the swings. Only three outdoor tables were occupied at the café in the old casino.

"How are you?" he asked, not moving an inch. I walked right up to him and leaned right next to him.

"I'm fine. How are you?" He looked down at me. "You wanted to see me?" I tried to mirror his pose and cross my arms. Somehow it just didn't feel relaxed or natural when I was doing it, but he made it look like he was born to lean on that bandstand.

"I was wondering if maybe you wanted to walk through the sculpture garden with me." He gestured to the outdoor sculpture garden across from us. The gates were wide open. I shook my head 'yes.'

We walked side by side down the sidewalk. At one point, he stopped and placed his hand on the small of my back, as we walked across the street. We entered the gates. The NOMA Sculpture Garden was completely deserted. The large oak trees made a canopy overhead, as we started on the path around a small pond.

"Good. I was hoping it would be empty." He reached into his back pocket and retrieved his phone. I waited as he clicked a button on the side of the phone. "All right, that's taken care of." He led me a little farther down the path. He leaned down and read one of the explanations of the works of art.

"Is there something here you wanted me to see?" I scanned the different pieces of art, trying to figure out what he wanted to show me.

"No, I just didn't want to be interrupted." He took my face between his palms and slowly lowered his lips to mine. There was no doubt about it, this was a kiss. Jason Stone was kissing me.

"What are you doing?" I asked Jason like an idiot. I knew what he was doing. Frankly, it was amazing.

"I don't know, but I want to keep doing it," he answered with a smile. Again he kissed me. Yep, things were definitely looking up.

THE END

ABOUT THE AUTHOR

 Like her main character Denise Reed, author Mary E. Koppel is a New Orleans' girl living right off Route 66! A mother, traveler and lover of mystery and romance, Mary is blessed with constant curiosity that has only gotten her into a little bit of trouble. She has written one book of essays, co-authored a book of non-fiction, and has written essays and devotions for blogs and publications. Mary's first Denise Reed mystery is *Volunteer to Die*.

www.ingramcontent.com/pod-product-compliance
Lightning Source LLC
Chambersburg PA
CBHW020333260626
47156CB00004B/1505